W9-BVL-836

Appleblossom the Possum

Appleblossom the Possum

BY

HOLLY GOLDBERG SLOAN

ILLUSTRATED BY

GARY A. ROSEN

Dial Books for Young Readers
an imprint of Penguin Group (USA) LLC

DIAL BOOKS FOR YOUNG READERS
Published by the Penguin Group
Penguin Group (USA) LLC
375 Hudson Street
New York, New York 10014

USA / Canada / UK / Ireland / Australia / New Zealand / India / South Africa / China

penguin.com

A Penguin Random House Company

Library of Congress Cataloging-in-Publication Data

Sloan, Holly Goldberg, date.
Appleblossom the possum / Holly Goldberg Sloan ; illustrated by Gary A. Rosen. pages cm
Summary: A young possum strikes out on her own and winds up trapped in a human house before her brothers can rescue her.
ISBN 978-0-8037-4133-1 (hardcover)
[1. Opossums—Fiction.] I. Rosen, Gary A., date, illustrator II. Title.

PZ7.S633136Ap 2015 [Fic]—dc23 2014039016

Manufactured in the USA

1 3 5 7 9 10 8 6 4 2

Designed by Mina Chung
Text set in Cooper Old Style

For Annie & Katie Kleinsasser, my first sisters

—H.G.S.

For Brother Bill

—G.A.R.

Appleblossom the Possum

Chapter 1

One moment she's calm and cozy with a knee in her nose and a tail around her neck.

And then push comes to shove and she's out!

But she doesn't have fur to keep her skin warm. And her eyes can't open, so there's nothing to see. She hears her brothers and sisters all take the gulp of new life and they don't sound happy. And then something speaks to her.

THUMP. THUMP. THUMP. THUMP. THUMP.

Her mother's beating heart tells her she should move.

Does a pounding beat *always* say that to a living thing?

The newborn possum babies need to get inside their mother's pouch. So she starts.

S l o w l y.

She is less than an inch long. The chill of the night air bites as she drags herself forward. (At her side, three other babies slip off the large belly and quiver in the mud below, so it's good that she can't see.) The wind rattles branches and shakes wet pine needles. A blue-eyed crow, on a perch in the distance, caws a warning.

But a dozen minutes later, when the tiny possum finally reaches the opening to her mother's pouch, she's out of energy. Her body trembles as her tiny hands and tiny feet, equipped with the tiniest of thumbs, grow numb.

Mama, I can't move.

There is no answer. Just the *THUMP, THUMP, THUMP* to advance.

Mama, I'm stuck.

Mama . . .

Ma?

Then luck is on her side because Mama Possum suddenly sits up and her pouch opens and gravity does the rest. The baby tumbles down,

down,

down.

The *THUMP, THUMP, THUMP* is louder here. And it's joined by *WHUMPs*. Many of them. They are fast and so familiar.

Whump. Whump. Whump. Whump. Whump. Whump. Whump. Whump. Whump. Whump. Whump. Whump.

Whump. Whump. Whump. Whump. Whump.

Are her brothers and sisters congratulating

her on making it inside? The heartbeats are like applause.

As she settles into the crowded, safe place, a tail wraps around her neck and a knee jabs her in the nose.

She understands they are all on this journey together.

Chapter 2

The babies of a first-time possum mother must have names that begin with the letter *A*. This explains to half sisters and half brothers, cousins and aunts, uncles, grandparents, and other relatives how they each fit into their own possum family.

Second-batch babies (according to possum tradition) use the letter *B*. Not many possum mothers reach *G*, but there's a clan on the edge of the city dump that claims enough litters for the babies to have *Z* names. There are rumors that they skipped ahead and there's no way of knowing for sure, but it's a fact that there is a group of possums at the dump named Zeke and Zack and Zelda and Zoe and Zita and Zalman and Zehra and Zeus and Ziggy, which makes them very, very special.

The A-babies recently born under a rotten log in the middle of a cold night live in their mother's pouch on a lifeline of liquid food. Their eyes open, their fur grows, and so do their bodies.

Two months later they are strong enough to be out in the world. Mama Possum is a free thinker and she encourages her babies to find their own names. So far there is an Antonio and an Alisa. Plus Abdul and Ajax and Alberta and Angie and Allan and Alphonse and Atticus and Alejandro and Augusta. And there is an Amlet (he wanted to be named Hamlet, but he wasn't an H-baby). But the last one to enter the pouch, the littlest possum that almost didn't make it to safety, still has no name.

She is seventy-seven days old and must learn

possum life, which means she is taking acting lessons. The other possums watch as she wiggles around on a patch of dirt. She's rehearsing being a snake.

Mama Possum, who is a natural theater director, instructs her: "Your tail looks believable. But you need to feel more like a snake in your body. Move from the inside."

The littlest possum raises her hand. Her question isn't about technique; while squirming, she has gotten distracted. That happens to her a lot. "I want everyone to know that there's something hatching above us on the tree," she says.

Antonio calls out, "Those are apple blossoms. And they don't hatch. They're flowers." Antonio has answers. He's just a natural born thinker.

Her brother Ajax starts to laugh. But not in a good way. "She thinks a flower is alive! *She's* an apple blossom."

Alberta giggles. "No, she's not!"

Mama Possum claps her hands together and that signals that it's time to take a break, or at the very least that Ajax should watch his mouthy attitude. But the littlest possum doesn't mind. She knows what Ajax said was meant as an insult, but she likes the way the word sounds: Appleblossom. She raises her voice so that they can all hear: "Today I take the name Appleblossom."

No one answers. So she adds, "Don't try calling me Allison."

Ajax sputters, "We won't."

And from that moment on, she is Appleblossom the possum.

It isn't long before the break is over and it's time to return to theater class. Appleblossom is happy that it's another possum's turn. Her eyes focus on her sister Angie. She doesn't have to be a snake. She's more advanced and she's doing a scene with Amlet. All of the possums are quiet. This is a very dramatic scene and Angie is a very dramatic possum. She puts her hand to her forehead and moans, "No. No. The drink! Oh, my dear Amlet. The drink, the drink. I am poisoned." Angie falls to the ground. Her breathing slows to next to nothing. Then her neck stiffens, her arms and legs extend straight out, and her tongue rolls from her mouth.

Appleblossom is horrified, but Mama

Possum claps and the rest of the group cheer. There's nothing these possum babies like more than to celebrate a worthy performance. And this is an excellent death scene!

Appleblossom's voice quivers with concern: "Are you sure Angie's okay? She really doesn't look good. Maybe we should check on her."

The smallest possum turns away. She has tears in her eyes. Mama tries to comfort her as she explains that "acting" is a vital part of being a possum.

But none of them has any idea why.

Chapter 3

Possums are born into darkness and they stay that way.

They are, as the thinker Antonio says, "nocturnal." And nocturnal things sleep during the day and are awake at night. There is a whole world of creatures that only appear when the sun goes down, and that means that the darkness is very much alive. Lots of birds, along with the small mice in the fields and the rats that creep out of the clumps of ivy and heaps of trash, are also nocturnal.

So are the bushy-tailed raccoons that come down from the hills after the sun sinks into the horizon. Skunks sleep until nightfall unfolds, snuggled underneath porches, or concealed behind rusty gardening tools stacked in the corner of backyards. Many types of spiders emerge from cracks in the bark of trees or the undersides of outdoor furniture only when the sky has gone dark.

Bats take to the air. Moths and black beetles edge away from the camouflage of mottled branches and pitted fences. Enterprising badgers squeeze out from openings behind trash cans and stacks of firewood. Deer hop over fences, entering yards to eat rosebushes and the newly green tops of hedges. Crickets and toads and frogs open their mouths and call out to announce the arrival of darkness.

But not one of these nocturnal animals is like a possum. Because as Mama Possum explains, "None of the other creatures are *marsupials*."

When they first hear this news, all of the possum babies cheer. Alberta starts a chant: "WE ARE MARSUPIALS! WE ARE MARSUPIALS! WE ARE MARSUPIALS!" All of the baby possums join in, and they make a *possumid,* which is a pyramid of possums. The cheering goes on for some time before Appleblossom stops to ask: "But what *is* a marsupial?"

The other babies fall silent. Even Antonio, who knows a lot because he likes to investigate, doesn't have this answer. Mama Possum explains: "Marsupials have pouches where their babies live after they are born. Kangaroos and koala bears are marsupials."

Amlet is confused. "What's a kangaroo or a koala bear?"

Mama Possum's long nose twitches. It does that when she's uncertain. "They don't live around here."

Appleblossom suddenly worries that the kangaroos and koala bears might be lost and need help. She asks, "Should we try to find the other marsupials?"

Mama Possum's ears point skyward in alarm. "No. Absolutely not! You should try to find snails, earthworms, eggs in nests, and fallen apples. Our job is clear. We spend our time digging for beetles and ant colonies. When that doesn't work, we sniff out birdfeeders stocked with seed. We do our best to remove chicken bones from trash cans and the uneaten remains from sticky wrappers flung to the ground. We are hunters, yes, but we are also great scavengers! We are the cleanup crew that comes in after the mess. And speaking of messes, there is no better place than a football field after a big game. Or at least that's what I've heard. We are *neighborhood* possums. This is our area. I've never actually been to a stadium parking lot after a sporting event, but from the chatter I hear, there's nothing like it."

Antonio raises his hand. He's just had an epiphany, which is like saying a light went off in his mind—but because they live in darkness, this is more like saying the shadows got bigger and so did his understanding.

Mama Possum looks pleased with her clever possum baby. "Yes, Antonio?"

"Being scavengers explains why we have so many teeth. With all the different food sources, we need a full jaw to grind the grub."

Murmurs of "grind the grub" circulate among the possum babies. They like the way it sounds. Mama Possum beams with happiness. "This is true, Antonio!"

Appleblossom points one of her fingers up into the sky and waits for her turn. Mama nods to her. "Go ahead, Appleblossom."

The littlest possum takes a moment to collect her thoughts. What she wants to say feels very important. "Having a full jaw means that we have great smiles!"

Appleblossom thinks she hears sneezing behind her. But when she turns around, Allan's making

a crazy face, and Alberta and Alisa are laughing.

Mama Possum stops the commotion. "Thank you for sharing, Appleblossom. Now I'm off to find our next meal. You possums stay together right here and do your improvisational exercises. I'm going to have each one of you stage something for me very soon. Remember, whatever you do, you have got to be convincing. Use your imagination! That's the key to a great performance."

And with that, Mama Possum disappears into an overgrown hedge and leaves her thirteen babies to rehearse. They are hopeful that she'll come back dragging a piece of rotten fruit or a paper sack with the remains of cold, greasy French fries.

Either option would be a truly tasty delight.

Chapter 4

They are nomads.

Or as Mama Possum explains: "Ours is a road show. At the end of every few nights we find a new sleeping spot. Some are better than others, but don't even think about hanging your hat and calling any place *home*."

Appleblossom wonders what that means, because they don't wear hats, although she would like to.

Now that they are out of the pouch, they travel on their mother's back whenever they relocate. All thirteen of them. And this always happens when the sun goes down. Mama Possum has rules, but one is more important than all the others put together. This one rule cannot be broken. Ever.

It's called bedtime.

Nothing matters more than following her exact instructions when Mama Possum says that it's time to burrow under a log, squeeze into a drainpipe, or slide under a seldom-used barbeque. When the sun starts to change the color of the dark sky to something close to a ripe plum, they know that they need to disappear.

Bodies safely hidden.

Then wide eyes shut.

All the nocturnal animals do the same thing. They vanish from view. The raccoons return to the hills. The bats find hollows in trees and rocks. The skunks slip away like magicians. The beetles and the moths simply stop moving.

Mama Possum's knowledge has been passed down from possum to possum. Now it's her turn to be a teacher. Darkness fully falls, and her babies, awake again, huddle in a circle. Her brood is three months old when she reveals her most important information: "We are awake only at night because when the sun is out, *monsters rule the world*."

Amlet was the last one to stop sucking his thumb, and now he can't help himself. He puts his whole hand in his mouth, but not before saying, "*Monsters?*"

Mama Possum tries to make her voice sound comforting, even though what she says isn't: "Yes. Now, there are three kinds of monsters, and all three kinds are terrifying. They are present at night, but they really own the day."

Appleblossom's brothers and sisters move closer to one another as Mama Possum continues: "The first kind of monster is made of metal. They have wheels and bright eyes when they are out after dark. These eyes are blinding."

Antonio interrupts. "We've heard the metal monsters before. They are loud!"

Mama Possum nods. "Yes, Antonio, the metal monsters roar. And honk. And they move very, very fast. They can flatten an animal in an instant if one gets in the way."

Appleblossom can't even think about something so frightening. She tries to close her ears, but it isn't like closing her eyes. She can still hear her mother's voice.

"The metal monsters are called cars and trucks.

The ones that live around here only go on certain paths. Some of these paths, ones far from here, are so wide and so filled with cars and trucks that at night they look like ribbons of white and red light. Only a fool would ever go near those huge metal monster paths. Only a fool, or someone with no other option."

Appleblossom promises herself to always stay away from the wide monster paths. Antonio makes a comment. "But the cars sleep. And then they are harmless as boulders. You've taken us near a car when its chest was cold and its eyes were dark."

Mama Possum rubs her hands together. "Yes, this is part of what you must learn. When is a car awake and when is it asleep?"

Appleblossom raises her hand. "So what we need to know is what wakes them up?"

It takes Mama Possum a long time to answer.

Her nose twitches and then she finally says, "The second kind of monster has formed an alliance with the cars and trucks. So our understanding of both enemies is important. The monsters work together. The *second* monster wakes up the first."

Amlet follows with, "What's the second kind of monster?"

Appleblossom asks, "What's an alliance?"

Mama Possum steadies herself. "Now is as good a time as ever to spill the beans."

Allan looks around. "What beans?"

Amlet gives him a small kick. "It's a saying, Allan. It means she's telling us the whole story."

Allan looks disappointed. "Oh. I like beans. Especially the dark ones that have spicy sauce."

Suddenly Appleblossom is very, very frightened. Mama Possum wraps her long tail around Appleblossom and pulls her close. "The second category of scary creatures walks on two feet. They smell like dead flowers, salt, and grease. Everything scares them. They are always angry. And they don't have tails."

Not having tails seems very sad to the babies. Angie shakes her head. She is dramatic and is ac-

knowledged now as being the best performer of the group. She strikes her signature pose, which is a hand to her forehead, as she wails, "An animal without a tail is so sad."

At her side Alisa adds, "Maybe that's why they are angry."

Whispers of "so sad" and "angry" buzz throughout the group. Mama Possum waits until they've quieted down and then continues. "The second monsters are called people. The people cover themselves in layers of cloth because they have very little fur. They scream when they see a night creature. They are noisy and unpredictable. They are dangerous, and not very smart, believe me!"

All of the possum babies stare at their mother. It's clear they do believe her.

"Now, the people don't like to share. That is their biggest problem. So they set traps, and they use weapons and poison. They are sneaky and mean. But the good part is that most of the time they don't climb trees at night. Or go into hedges or dig holes."

Sighs of relief come from the babies. And they are big sighs.

Mama Possum adds: "The people are awake for part of the night, but they go into their houses and stare at boxes there."

Appleblossom is confused. "What kind of boxes?"

Mama Possum's eyes narrow. "The boxes have light and sound, and the people watch these contraptions for hours. Some of the light boxes hang on the walls of the houses. Some are just off the ground. And others are held right in their hands."

Antonio waves his tail. "I think the light boxes might be telling the monsters what to do."

Mama Possum looks as if she's giving this idea

some thought, but the discussion is over and no one objects when she says, "We've had enough for one night."

Appleblossom can't fall asleep after her mother's Big Talk. The world's a scary place, and she needs to learn so much to stay safe. She isn't sure that she's up to the job. Her acting skills aren't as advanced as her brothers' and sisters'. She doesn't have any special talents like dancing or singing or speaking with an accent. She's good at smelling night-blooming jasmine, and watching the bats swirl in the dark sky as they circle the streetlight. She's good at observing the world. Does that count?

In the distance, the sun edges up over the treetops and Appleblossom feels her tail tremble. Her whole family is hidden in a mildewy umbrella that's on its side in a garden not far from where she now realizes people live. At a distance on one of the paths is a car. It isn't moving. But that doesn't make her feel any better.

Appleblossom squeezes her eyes shut and tries to make the bad thoughts go away, when Antonio whispers, "Appleblossom, I'm awake."

Appleblossom whispers back: "I'm afraid."

"Me too," he says.

A few moments later, another voice says, "I'm not afraid, but I can't sleep either." It's Amlet. Appleblossom wonders if he's just acting brave right now or if he's being truthful. He's a very good actor.

Appleblossom doesn't want to cry; she might wake everyone up. Or worse, she might wake up a monster. "So what do we do?" she asks.

Antonio whispers back to her, "We watch out for each other. I'll keep my eye on you two. And you do the same."

Appleblossom's mouth wobbles into a small smile. "We could snuggle closer."

Amlet pushes his way in between Antonio and Appleblossom. "Good idea. You two can be lookouts. I'll handle the middle." Appleblossom and Antonio are quiet, but they feel better.

And before they know it, all three possums are sound asleep.

Chapter 5

Several nights pass before Mama Possum decides it's time for more training. While her thirteen little ones chew on a special snack—an eight-inch-long, slimy, salty, yellow-green slug—she gets down to business. "Tonight we learn about the last kind of monster. The worst kind of monster. Our greatest enemy."

Appleblossom stops eating. "What could be worse than the people and the cars and trucks?"

Mama says, "A group known as the hairies."

The little possums erupt into an explosion of overlapping voices:

"The hairies?"

"The scaries!"

"Or the maraschino cherries!"

Antonio is the one who brought up the cherries. No one else has any idea what he's talking about. Mama waits until they quiet down and then explains. "There are many types of hairies."

Appleblossom looks at her brothers and sisters. "Are we hairies?"

Mama's eyes get wide. "We are marsupials that have hair! That's very different." She exhales and continues.

"Cats are a single category of hairies, but I'm not going to bother with them because you are big enough now to fend them off. The hairies that can ruin our lives are known as dogs."

The baby possums absorb the word *dog*. It does have a hard sound to it.

Mama continues. "These creatures are the sworn enemy of all possums, big and small, young and old, weak and strong. Dogs are covered in fur. They have tails and can dig. They move on four feet and they have sharp teeth and they use them. And unlike people, these monsters are not filled with fear. Dogs are highly unpredictable and can appear in the daytime *or* at night. In a single lunge a dog can rip off your head. That's what kind of a threat they are."

Amlet and Angie and Alberta and Ajax and Abdul and Allan and Alphonse and Atticus and Alejandro and Alisa and Augusta and Antonio and Appleblossom hook tails. This is very bad news.

Antonio speaks for the group: "Do dogs make noise? Do we hear them coming?"

Mama Possum looks relieved. "Yes, Antonio. Dogs bark. But you can't count on that to warn you." She points to a house in the distance. "There is some good news, though. Dogs are very needy and don't live by themselves. They have relationships with people. But not all people have dogs. You must learn which houses have dogs. You must avoid those places."

Appleblossom feels a little bit better. She can tell that Antonio and Amlet do too.

Most of the others bounce back completely. Alejandro hooks his arm through Augusta's and they twirl around. Augusta squeals, "We find the people without the dogs and we stay away from the cars and the trucks and then the show can begin!"

Mama Possum puts a stop to the dancing. "No! It's not that simple. Dogs are the worst of the worst. They keep a possum from drifting off to sleep as the sun comes up, because behind every closed gate, the dog could be waiting."

Appleblossom's voice isn't much more than a whisper: "So what do we do?"

For the first time, Mama Possum smiles. "We die."

The possums exchange looks. What is she talking about? Mama continues. "Dogs like *live* things much, much, much more than *dead* things."

Alphonse raises his tail. "I don't understand. Are you saying we don't put up a fight?"

Mama Possum lowers her voice. They all lean in. "That's right. We do not fight. We do not run. Dogs are always bigger, faster, and stronger than we are. But, as I was saying, if they see a dead thing, they stop. They investigate, but with caution. They do *not* like dead things."

Appleblossom's voice is small. "Why? We eat dead things."

Mama sighs. "We can't compare ourselves to them. We are a higher life form. People feed dogs. It's part of their evil alliance. And there are people and dogs who kill for sport."

All of the baby possums start talking at once: *"Who kills for sport? They're monsters, all right! They are the most awful of the awful."*

Mama Possum quiets them down by waving her arms in the air. "So now you see why I ask you over and over again to learn to act. This is how we trick them. We *act* dead. But we aren't really dead. It's an art form. It *must* look real."

Amlet's chest puffs out and he bellows in a loud

and showy voice, "To be or not to be. That is the question!"

Mama Possum smiles again. "Yes, Amlet! Well done!"

Appleblossom looks down at her feet. She doesn't practice acting as much as she should. But Mama Possum is reassuring. "Don't worry, little ones. Part of our fake-dying is out of our control. In the event of a true crisis, instinct takes over and we *look* stricken because we *are* stricken."

Antonio adds, "So fear makes you feel like you really are having a heart attack?"

Mama Possum explains: "When something really, truly scares us, all kinds of things happen. Our lungs slow down. Our arms and legs go limp and then they turn stiff. Our eyes fall shut. And for some of us, our tongues roll out and spit starts bubbling from the corners of our mouths." A smile spreads across Mama Possum's face. There's more good news to share. "The final touch is smell. Dead things stink. That's just a fact. And to add to the illusion of death, we possums can release a gas. A real stink bomb."

The possums get all giggly as relief washes over them like a warm dip in a backyard birdbath.

Mama Possum adds: "The stink gas is one of our most important gifts. It tricks dogs and people into thinking that we are yesterday's news. Dead is dead. Only in our case, dead isn't dead. Dead is the only way to stay alive."

Mama Possum raises her arms wide and high and spreads her fingers. "So you see, my beautiful babies, we are the true performers of the animal kingdom. We are the stars!"

Chapter 6

Gland gas.

It's just that simple. A possum can lift her tail and release foul air, and it gives her a better chance to survive when in danger. Playing dead is one thing. But *smelling* dead is another. It adds a whole other layer to a possum performance. The gland gas is a special effect. And a special effect can enhance even a very dull act.

All of the A-babies now want to work every waking moment on their acting techniques. So for the next few days the possums spend as much time as possible performing tense and scary scenes. And for the first time, Appleblossom excels. It turns out that being the easiest to frighten can come in handy.

Once her brothers and sisters see how fun it is to make Appleblossom go numb, they all want to be part of her show. On seven different occasions Appleblossom collapses to the ground, arms stiff to the night sky. She is terrific at fainting and releasing an awful smell, because to her it's all real.

Mama watches and is very proud. "All of you should observe Appleblosom's technique. You will see that she is free and bold in her performing choices. She doesn't hold back. Great acting involves preparation and then an authentic response."

Angie raises her hand. "Could Appleblossom explain her process? Could she give us pointers?"

Appleblossom's face grows hot with embarrass-

ment. "I really can't say how I'm doing it. I keel over because I'm completely in the moment."

Mama Possum gushes with excitement. "That's how good you are! Actors find a way to be open to the world! They channel emotion! Keep your eye on your little sister. She's going places."

A week later, Mama Possum has a new lesson planned for her babies. After waking them, she feeds the group a good breakfast consisting of eight snails (two in broken shells), three worms (still alive), a variety of seeds purloined from a birdfeeder, and a pile of mushy coffee grounds (good for digestion) trapped in a hardened paper filter. She insists that they take turns and everyone gets part of the prize, and then she makes an announcement.

"There are car paths all around us. I navigate these areas all the time, and tonight you will take the stage and cross. One by one. Alone."

Appleblossom raises her hand. "What if we don't think we're ready yet?"

Mama Possum's nose twitches. "You're ready."

Appleblossom is anxious. "But—"

Mama Possum turns back to the group. "Even if you aren't ready, *act* ready. Each of you will take a turn. Stage fright can be overcome. Fake it until you make it, possums."

Appleblossom can't stop herself; she whispers to Antonio, "I'm never crossing."

Mama Possum hears her. "You already have. Many times. But you were in my pouch and didn't know what was happening. So it's true to say that you have all done this before."

Antonio feels it necessary to add: "Yes, but not by ourselves."

Mama Possum tries to be patient. "I remember

the first time I crossed a car path. I was very afraid, but I did it. And you can do it. The most important thing about crossing is timing."

Amlet tries to be the bravest performer and shouts out, "I will make the first entrance. I'm not afraid of stepping out onto a car path!"

But instead of being pleased, Mama Possum looks angry. "No, Amlet! You *must* be afraid. And for very, very, very good reason. A car is too large and too powerful for any possum to ever challenge. Playing dead doesn't work for these monsters. They run right over dead things. They even slam straight into each other!"

Amlet's nose twitches and his eyes slide off into the distance. His chest isn't as puffy as before. If he's acting hurt, he's doing a good job.

Mama Possum raises her tail and commands: "Form a line."

Angie shouts with her trademark excitement, "A chorus line?"

Mama Possum shakes her head. "Not this time, Angie."

Appleblossom moves to the back of the group as they assemble. Antonio takes the place right in front of her. Amlet stays in the front. After a lot of pushing and shoving, they manage to find some kind of order.

Overhead, a full moon suddenly pokes through the clouds. It's so bright that Appleblossom can see her shadow. And it's shaking.

Mama Possum glances up at the sky and mutters to herself: "Too much moon." But a moment later her eyes settle on the wide cement path. No cars can be heard, so Mama heads out into the open. She stops in the middle of the path and then rises up so that she's balancing on her back legs. "The show must go on! Now one at a time. Look both ways before you cross! Amlet, you want to be first. Take the stage when you are ready!"

Appleblossom is too nervous to watch. So she turns her head and stares up into the night sky.

Amlet doesn't prepare. He doesn't center himself. He doesn't do a single breathing exercise. Or even look both ways. He just starts running. His whole body wiggles as he scrambles out into the wide cement path. He's halfway across when Appleblossom screams, "NO, AMLET! WATCH OUT!"

All of the babies (except for Amlet) look up to see a shape in the sky. It's large and has wings and is headed right for Amlet. Angie and Alberta and Ajax and Abdul and Allan and Alphonse and Augusta and Alejandro and Alisa and Atticus dive into the ivy. Antonio and Appleblossom hold hands and run into a drainpipe.

But Amlet, intent on his performance, keeps moving.

The moonlight reveals that the flying attacker's feet are bony, with hooked sharp ends. Right before they sink into Amlet's spine, Mama throws herself on top of Amlet and he slams to the ground. The claws of the villain come down on the back of a full-size possum, not a lightweight baby. Mama lets out a single, awful scream and the flapping maniac lifts his head and releases.

All is not lost.

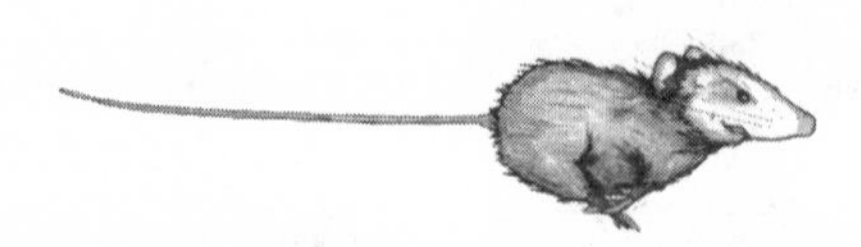

Chapter 7

They are called owls.

And these night criminals are just one more thing for the A-babies to add to a terrifying list that keeps getting longer and longer. But the good news is that as they get older and bigger, these enemies will no longer be a problem.

Amlet survives the attack, with a bruised nose and sore knees and a permanent crimp in his tail, but the cement path show is closed after the incident and no further performances are scheduled.

Amlet is changed after that night. Appleblossom notices that he becomes a different kind of actor. He never again puffs out his chest and shouts, "To be or not to be!" He's more of an ensemble player after the owl incident and he stays close to Appleblossom. He is, as he explains, "filled with self-doubt."

Mama Possum doesn't complain even once about the wounds on her back. She says that it's the moon's fault. Everyone is vulnerable in a spotlight. "So there's another lesson to be learned: Pay attention to the moon and the stars. The importance of lighting can make or break a performance."

A week passes and they all do their best to forget about the villains known as owls, and the moon that can be too much of a spotlight. Now Mama Possum doesn't give much instruction when they follow her up a tree or ride on her back. She's quiet and her eyes focus into the distance on something they can't see. She's there and not there.

Not many nights later, it's windy with a half-moon when Mama Possum makes an announcement: "Tonight we separate and put on our own shows."

All the A-possums are alarmed. They are never solo acts; that's one of the rules of an ensemble company. They stay together no matter what happens. Mama continues: "Tonight I want you to strike out and find your *own* food. This is no dress rehearsal. I need you to show me how skilled you are!"

Allan pulls his tail around his tummy and his waist gets small. He keeps it this way like a belt (even though it looks very uncomfortable) as he asks, "Why can't we do that as a troupe? We are community players and we—"

Mama stops him. "You are big enough. You are strong enough. You are ready for center stage."

Mama's voice changes; it gets soft and sounds suddenly sad. "Now, I've told you many stories about the good times growing up with my sisters Carlotta and Crissy." The babies nod. "And we were in the woods when we all came upon my sister Cherry." The babies nod again. "But I don't live with Carlotta and Crissy and Cherry. And I haven't seen Campy or Clementine or Cotty since we were small. Cotty said he wanted to perform on a big screen, so I imagine he went through with it."

The babies wait as she finally continues: "I left a rotten pear this year during the holidays in the drainpipe where we were born. It took most of the night to get over there. If it hadn't been rain-ing, it would have been easier. I made a bow out of a strand of spaghetti and I placed it on top. But I never heard back from anyone. We are family; there's no changing that. Even if I don't get to see much of them."

The babies don't move a muscle.

Then Antonio whispers to Appleblossom: "She's reminiscing."

Appleblossom leans close. "Is it acting?"

Antonio keeps his voice low. "It's thinking back on the good times. You don't usually need to act to do that."

But Mama Possum doesn't speak any more about her brothers or sisters or where they are or the pear wrapped in a spaghetti bow that no one thanked her for. And she doesn't bring up her own mama. Or her own papa.

Instead, she swings her large body around so

that the babies can only see her tail as she says, "You know what to do. You were born to be actors. Tonight, act brave. Stay out of street light. Stay away from all light, for that matter. Be alert. Don't talk to strangers, especially skunks. And look both ways if you decide to take the cement path." She starts to walk away.

Angie steps forward. She half wails what they all are thinking: "But Mama, what about the monsters?"

Mama Possum keeps moving. Her voice is thick like maybe she swallowed something too big and it got stuck. "Make sure to be asleep when the sky turns purple. There's nothing more important."

Mama Possum lifts her head high into the air and they see the top of her nose twitch. "Should danger strike, remember to play possum. All the world's a stage."

And without looking over her shoulder, Mama slips into the ivy and is gone.

The young possums are wide-eyed.

Before Amlet was almost eaten by the owl, he would have shouted that he wasn't afraid to go off by himself. But now he just stands silently in the shadows and stares at the place where his mother had been standing.

Antonio takes a deep breath and speaks to his brothers and sisters. He hopes that he sounds reassuring. "Mama's right. We've rehearsed. We know what to do. We're ready for this."

Alisa's upper lip curls and she shows all her teeth. But it isn't a smile. It's too shaky for that. She ordinarily isn't much of a talker, but she sounds tough as she says, "All right then. I'm gonna roll." And before anyone can answer, she wiggles away into the darkness and disappears.

Atticus can't stop himself: "I'm going to tell Mama."

Allan's dark, intense eyes fall on his brother. "What are you going to tell her?"

Atticus looks sad. "She didn't say a proper good-bye."

The words hang in the air.

Is he talking about Alisa or about Mama Possum?

No one dares to ask.

Chapter 8

They are all hungry and there's nothing to do but go look for something to eat.

Slowly, the group starts to break apart. Abdul and Allan head off to investigate the hillside where a group of trees have sticky bark. It catches flies and unsuspecting gnats.

Alejandro and Angie and Atticus decide to go dig for treasure down in a field not far away. They think they smell something rotten buried there under a pile of dead branches.

Alphonse announces that he's going to investigate the often stagnant stream by the sycamore trees. He believes it holds the promise of little toads and slimy salamanders. Ajax and Augusta and Alberta look confused as they wander off in different directions.

Amlet's tail still has a crimp in the middle from the calamity on the cement path. It causes him to walk with a small hitch in his step. He moves forward a few feet into the darkness, but turns back. He then looks at his brother and sister. "I'm not afraid. But I do feel attached to the two of you. Especially Appleblossom."

Appleblossom's nose wrinkles up. "Don't pick favorites."

Amlet shrugs. "Just saying. No offense meant."

Antonio mumbles, "None taken."

Appleblossom grabs her tail and holds it tight. "You two go. I'll wait here."

Amlet looks at Antonio. "Okay, then I'll tag along with you, Antonio. Just to keep you company." But Antonio doesn't answer.

A warm wind blows hard from the north. Appleblossom shouldn't be cold, but she feels the hair stand up on her back. Antonio looks right at her and says, "Appleblossom, you should come with us."

The littlest possum shakes her head. Antonio is more insistent. "Please? Aren't you hungry?"

Appleblossom whispers, "Antonio, I'm not acting right now. I can't. I just want to stay here." Antonio knows she really means it. He reaches out to reassure her.

It isn't clear whether Amlet is performing, but he puts a hand on Appleblossom's shoulder and says, "We'll stay close—right, Antonio? We'll be in the wings. We'll be watching."

Antonio finally turns to go, whispering, "I'm not going to say good-bye because I'm coming back soon."

Appleblossom shuts her eyes, but when she opens them moments later, her brothers haven't gone far. Antonio and Amlet are looking back at her from the shadows.

Antonio lifts his tail high in the air and makes it sway. Appleblossom pulls herself up onto her hind legs to make herself tall. She raises her right arm and waves back. And then Antonio spins around and scurries off into the grass, with Amlet at his heels.

Appleblossom's mind races. *I'm not ready to put on my own show. The most important thing right now isn't finding something to eat; it's finding a safe place. Cars don't climb trees, and dogs don't do more than jump and snap at lower limbs. People only go up trees when the sun's out and they have tools in their hands. Or at least that's what Mama Possum said. Maybe if I climb a tree I can look down at my brothers and sisters and maybe even see Mama Possum.*

In the distance she hears the sound of a car. The glow from the eyes of the beast lights up the world. It motivates her.

Appleblossom gathers all her courage and goes. But she can't see Antonio or Amlet; the grass is too tall. She considers calling out to them, but making noise at night is risky business. So she stays along the edge of the bushes, and does not venture out in the wide-open space (which is the most dangerous place for any creature to be).

Before she knows it, she is at the base of the tree in the yard next to a house. No owl has appeared from the sky and lifted her away for a meal. No dog has ripped off her head. She feels a wave of relief as she scrambles up the trunk into the shelter of the leaves.

Appleblossom's sharp nails dig into the bark and her skill surprises her as she ascends toward the crown of the enormous tree. She doesn't stop even once. She might be the smallest of the A-baby possums, but she's determined and she has good balance.

Appleblossom climbs higher and higher, passing dozens of branches and even a small hole where she spies the remains of a bird's nest. Finally she is at the top. There she wraps her tail around a thin branch for safety.

Appleblossom turns her gaze upward. She sees the starry night as a field of tiny lights. On the distant horizon she locates the blurry edge of an orange moon. As her heart slows and her breathing returns to normal, Appleblossom decides there is

only one thing to do when she's afraid to perform: She has to always move forward, even if she feels small and alone in the world and not much of an actor.

She has to find a role she can play.

Chapter 9

It turns out that there are things to eat high up in the treetops.

Appleblossom hears buzzing and looks over at a moth. She has eaten moths before, and while they are often dusty-dry and bitter to the taste, they have a nice crunch. So Appleblossom grabs the insect and pops it into her mouth.

And as often happens, she doesn't realize how hungry she is until she starts chewing.

She finishes the moth and sees just inches away a slug, moving slowly down the tree branch and leaving a trail of thick goo. This is a prize! Appleblossom pulls on the slug. It stretches long and thin, but she is stronger than the suction and it pops off.

Dee-licious!

No other way to describe it. She decides to investigate other areas of the tree, and she is rewarded for the effort. Two limbs down she finds a cankerworm. What follows are a Japanese beetle, a leaf miner, a tent caterpillar, a fruit worm, and a line of red termites. Finally, hours later she hits upon her greatest discovery: a long-abandoned beehive. Inside are honey and pollen, as well as still-moist larvae trapped in hundreds of small chambers. She has never eaten anything so sweet and satisfying! The tree is a buffet of tasty treats.

But it is also a trap.

Because as Appleblossom savors the beehive, she loses track of time. And when she finally takes notice, it is too late. The black is gone from the sky and pink is seeping up on the horizon. The sun is only minutes from climbing out of the hills.

Appleblossom argues with herself. Should she try to go down the tree or will it take too long to get to the ground? If she made it, could she squeeze behind a woodpile or find her way back to the mulberry hedge?

Every moment she struggles to make a decision is an opportunity lost.

And then the shadows give way to the full illumination of the now terrifying world. What will become of her? She is high off the ground in a tree, but exposed to monsters (at least if they look up).

And then her worst fear happens.

A door opens on the house and a dog is released!

Appleblossom watches as the monster charges into the grassy area and heads straight for the tree. She tightens her grip into the bark and does her best not to move a muscle. Down below she sees the hairy creature lift his back leg and shoot liquid right at the tree. And then the dog puts his nose to the ground and sniffs.

What follows is highly unexpected. At least from Appleblossom's point of view. After a few sniffs the dog abruptly stops his investigation of the tree and moves to a round red ball that is in the grass. He uses his mouth to pick it up.

Mama Possum has taught her babies about balls.

They come in all colors and sizes, but they aren't

food and can't be eaten. Like most of the things the people make, balls are useless. But that doesn't stop the people from throwing them and hitting them with sticks and tossing them into nets. According to Mama, it is the saddest thing. For hours on end people watch other people chase balls on their light boxes.

Now Appleblossom's eyes stay on the dog with the red ball wedged in his jaw. He starts to run in circles around the yard. He gallops hard and fast, covering as much area as possible. He runs and runs and runs, and then the door of the house opens again.

The dog stops running.

And one of the people appears.

Appleblossom holds her breath. This is a close encounter of the real kind. Right below her is one of the other most dangerous monsters in the world!

Appleblossom strains to get a good look, and sees the brown fur on top of the people's head.

The creature is not big.

And does not look very scary.

Mama Possum has explained that the people control the dogs. Well, Mama is right, because the dog runs to the people and drops the ball at her feet. Then the dog takes off, zigging and zagging around in a crazy way.

The people shouts the words "Columbo, come here! Forget the ball." The voice is firm, but does not sound angry.

The dog stops and locks eyes with the people. It is some kind of standoff.

The dog moves first.

He runs back and picks up the ball with his mouth and then he drops it again. And then the dog sits down. And sort of cries. At least that's what it sounds like to Appleblossom. A small whimper.

Little Appleblossom forgets that she is scared. Now she is just interested. She watches as the people walks straight out into the dew-covered grass and picks up the red ball. The dog jumps to his feet as his mouth opens and he makes a high-pitched noise filled with anticipation. The people throws the red ball. It sails through the air, then hits a wooden fence and bounces back into a bush.

And the dog goes insane.

He runs after the red ball at an intense speed and then dives into the shrubs headfirst. He emerges only seconds later with the red ball again in his mouth. His eyes are now wild and he is so excited that he runs in circles, his head held high and his long ears flapping.

But by this point the people has moved back to the house. The people shouts, "No more ball."

Appleblossom watches as the dog slows down. She believes he is acting, because he looks really heart-broken. He is a very strong actor. He finally drops the useless red ball and goes to the people. The people then leans down and pats the head of the dog, and Appleblossom can see a look of kindness.

The people has to know how hopeless the dog

is and she is taking pity on him. Or else rewarding his performance.

And then the people returns to her house and the dog follows, but not before looking one last time (with real emotion) at the useless red ball.

Chapter 10

Antonio and Amlet are the first possums back to the mulberry hedge. They arrive a good hour before sunrise and Antonio carries a large, plump tomato in his mouth. His many teeth have punctured the red skin of the tasty treat, and juice drips from the corners of his mouth. He drops the prize with great relief as he calls out: "Appleblossom!"

No one answers.

Amlet shouts, using his full acting voice, which he hopes sounds commanding and filled with authority: "Appleblossom the possum! We're back."

Still no one answers. "She's missing her entrance," says Amlet. He and Antonio were certain that they would find her waiting just where they left her, and that she would be hungry.

The two possums look all around the hedge and Antonio even makes the bold move of scurrying out into the open to investigate a row of newly planted marigolds. But there is no sign of the littlest possum.

After conducting a thorough search, they return to the hedge and the tomato. Before, the vegetable was some kind of treasure. Now it is a sagging reminder that their smallest sister is missing.

Antonio rests his head in defeat against the tomato like a pillow. Amlet takes a seat next to him. And that's where they are when Atticus and Allan and Alberta and Alisa and Ajax and Abdul and Augusta and Alphonso and Alejandro return. They have dined on the skins of avocados and the rinds of moldy cheese. They have chewed on fried fish tails and potato peels and the cores of rotting crab apples. Antonio and Amlet listen to everyone's stories of the night, but they are both only thinking about Appleblossom. And then the sky starts the change over to day.

They all squeeze together behind a rusty metal bin that is near the hedge. No people has been near it for a long time. Augusta looks around and wonders, "Where's Mama?"

But no one knows. Like Appleblossom and Angie, Mama has not come back. The A-babies are exhausted from their first night alone. Minutes later, only Amlet and Antonio are awake (but hidden) when the sun comes up. Amlet whispers to Antonio: "Mama didn't come back to check on us."

Antonio takes some time before he answers. "No. But she's probably watching us."

This cheers up Amlet. "Really, you think so?"

"Yes. I'm certain." Antonio hopes that he is convincing.

Amlet looks pleased. "So it's some kind of test to see how we get along without her. Thanks for telling me, Antonio. I didn't know."

Amlet's voice is sleepier now. "Maybe Ap-pleblossom is watching with Mama. Maybe she's the lucky one."

Chapter 11

The world of daytime is loud and much more chaotic than the night.

Appleblossom has never been this tired, but she tries her hardest to stay awake. It helps that there are so many intriguing things to see. It is still early in the morning when an enormous yellow metal monster appears. It isn't a car or a truck, but it must be a family member of those beasts. The monster stops in front of the house and its red eyes flash in the front and the back. The same little people who earlier was with the dog named Columbo comes out of the house and goes to the yellow metal monster.

Appleblossom studies the creature as she walks. The people has brown fur on the top of her head that is now tied back with a red bow. She has large eyes that are the color of the little pebbles lining the stream through the canyon up in the hills. They are brown, but bright swirls of something close to green are there too.

There are other people inside the metal monster. Some of them wave their arms as the little monster from the house approaches. The people laughs. She is acting happy. Appleblossom listens. The monster's giggle is delicate. And it certainly doesn't sound like it belongs to an animal that is mean and ferocious. No. The little monster sounds sweet.

The metal monster opens his mouth and the people climbs inside. Then the yellow monster closes his mouth and moves away down the cement stage and Appleblossom finds herself sad to see the people go.

As the day progresses the dog comes out two more times. He has a routine, which involves lifting his leg, running in circles, and communicating with the red ball. The only other activity he undertakes is sniffing the ground. Vigorously. And yet he never once cranes his head and looks up. If he did, then he would see the small possum clinging to one of the top branches of the tree.

He is, Appleblossom decides, not a very complex life form.

The sun is higher in the sky when the yellow metal monster returns. The little people gets out, and Appleblossom watches as she makes her way back to the house. She stops before the entrance and leans over some purple flowers. Appleblossom feels certain that the little monster has caught sight of a juicy caterpillar or maybe a plump spider.

But this isn't the case. The people pushes her face close to the petals and simply inhales. She smells the sweetness. Appleblossom wants to shout from the treetop: "I love flowers too!" But she doesn't dare. And then the little monster plucks one of the blossoms and disappears into the house. Appleblossom waits for the rest of the daylight to see the little people again, but this doesn't happen.

It takes a long, long, long time for the sun to work its way across the sky and slip below the distant hills. But finally night falls. Appleblossom makes certain that the dog has just been out to chase his red ball, and, once he is back inside, she starts down the tree trunk.

Appleblossom appreciates the fact that she has thumbs! She can pick up snails and pill bugs and sweet fallen apples. Watching the dog use his mouth for everything has been an eye-opener. All he can do with his clumsy feet is scratch at the ground and send dirt flying in all directions. It's possible, she decides, that not having proper hands and feet is what makes him run in circles.

Appleblossom has survived a big test. She has

stayed out all day, and now returns to the mulberry bush with her head held high.

Antonio sees her first. His ears shoot skyward as he springs up on his back feet to get a better look. "Appleblossom!" he shouts. He and Amlet are waiting in the exact spot where they had all been the night before.

"What happened? You didn't come back!"

"It was horrible and scary and also incredible and amazing. Is that possible?"

Antonio grins and almost all of his fifty teeth can be seen. "If you say so, then it is."

"Was Mama mad at me for not being here for bedtime?"

Antonio isn't sure how to answer, but Amlet blurts out: "Mama wasn't here either. We thought you might be together."

Appleblossom is surprised that Mama didn't come back, but she sits down to tell her brothers everything that she has seen and experienced. She talks about the people and the dog and the red ball. She speaks until she can't form another sentence. With her brothers at her side, she finally has to drag herself to the mildewy umbrella against the wooden fence. The folds of the rotting canvas are like a hammock, and it is there, with her tail curled into a pillow, that she falls asleep. She is nocturnal, but she sleeps through the long night and all through the next day.

She is cozy and safe and, most of all, alive.

Chapter 12

Atticus and Allan and Alisa and Alberta and Ajax and Abdul haven't been seen in four nights.

Then Augusta and Alejandro don't come back after Alphonse disappears.

And Mama has not been spotted by anyone.

Even once.

The only reason they know that something awful hasn't happened to her is that twice when they return at the end of the night there is a piece of bruised fruit underneath the mulberry bushes. And both times, it is tied with a bow made from a strand of spaghetti.

Two days later, when the full moon begins to roll up the sky to let the sun peek over the hills, only Antonio and Amlet and Appleblossom wait in the meeting place under the mulberry hedge.

Appleblossom's forehead scrunches up and her eyes get cloudy as they fill with tears. "It's just the three of us now."

Amlet slips his head out of the leaves to look out into the grass, which he knows is dangerous in the low light. He doesn't see anyone coming. "What do you think happened to everybody?" He chews on a scrap of sticky stuff that he found flattened on the cement, and then answers his own question: "They moved on. That's what happened."

Appleblossom's whole body tenses. "But I don't understand why. We're family."

Antonio's voice is sad. "We can't keep coming back to this mulberry hedge. Animals can smell us.

Amlet, you were right. The others have moved on. And we're making a mistake by not following."

Amlet suddenly gets stubborn. "Well, what if I don't want to move on? What if I want to ride on Mama's back? What if I want to work on my performances? What if I want us to put on a show?"

Appleblossom looks at Amlet and tries her best to sound hopeful. "Just the three of us could run through the acting exercises. We could still workshop a scene."

Amlet's voice is but a whisper. "I'm not acting right now. My sadness is real."

Antonio scratches an itchy spot on top of his head. Appleblossom knows he does this when he's thinking hard. Finally he says: "We have to accept that it's just us now. And who knows how long *that* will even last?"

Appleblossom answers. "Forever. That's how long. You two are my brothers forever."

Antonio sighs. "But we are solitary animals. That's how it works."

Appleblossom looks down at her hands as if something important is happening there. Finally she stops staring at her thumbs and asks, "Says who? We don't have to be solitary if we don't *want* to be solitary."

Amlet looks at Antonio. "Can you explain what solitary is again?"

Antonio is, as always, patient. "It means just one. It means solo."

Appleblossom's eyes fill with liquid. "I don't see why we can't be solo together."

Antonio doesn't have an answer. Amlet chimes in, "Why can't we meet up at the end of every night? What's the harm in that? We can look for food on our own. Then come back here when we are done."

Antonio takes a long time to answer. "We can for now." Amlet and Appleblossom both let out sighs of relief. "But we need to be extra-careful. Three of us together means it's more difficult to find safe places to sleep. And we're getting bigger all the time. We can't just rely on what has worked before."

Appleblossom looks at her brothers. It's true that they are all growing fast. Their bellies are large and their tails are now so long. But instead of pointing this out, she says, "Of course, Antonio. We don't need to sleep in that old umbrella. We'll find a new place."

Amlet nods in agreement. "Whatever you say, Antonio. That's how we'll do it."

The three possums waste no time. They find a drainpipe that looks dry and they crawl inside as

Antonio leads the way. But a brown snake has already claimed the spot and the reptile makes an awful face. He sticks his purple tongue out and hisses in their direction. "No vacancy!" He gets his message across.

The possums scurry and take refuge inside an old tire that has been abandoned under the ivy on the hillside. They huddle next to one another in a cozy ball. The sun is cracking the horizon when Appleblossom whispers to her brothers, "There was room for all of us in that drainpipe even with the snake there. But if you're not wanted, there's no amount of space that will make a difference." And Antonio and Amlet agree.

Chapter 13

After twelve hours of rest, the three A-possums wake up to the splendor of a new dark night. They make a plan to meet by a gopher hole under an oleander shrub. Then they separate to seek their fortune, which means to find a good breakfast, lunch, and dinner.

Appleblossom keeps her long nose to the ground as she hunts for tasty pill bugs and earwigs and beetle grubs. She uses her hands and feet to pull up weeds and lift stones. She surprises herself an hour later when she realizes that she's somehow in the grassy yard where the dog lives with the little pebble-eyed people.

She knows that she should be afraid, but she can see the red ball in the shadows of the grass and that means that the dog is inside. In the dark she can see the house more clearly. The lights are on, and she makes out two very large monsters who are staring at a magic light box on the wall. Then the small people comes into the room. She doesn't look at the box. She turns and stares out the dark, see-through glass. Appleblossom doesn't dare move. What if the littlest monster screams and shouts and alerts the big people? What if the dog finds out she's in his yard?

Appleblossom holds her breath as the little creature walks closer to the glass. And then the monster does the craziest thing. She raises her hand and she waves.

Appleblossom pulls herself up onto her hind legs so that she's standing tall, and she raises her front paw and waves back. Appleblossom can see

that the little people is very happy. She's now smiling and laughing, and the two monsters staring at the light box turn to see what's going on.

This scares Appleblossom, and she drops to the ground and takes off for the cover of the bushes. She runs until she's out of breath. But when she finally stops running, she is happy too. She likes the little people. They both appreciate flowers.

At the end of the night, Appleblossom meets up with Antonio and Amlet and they find an excellent sleeping spot inside a cinder block wall. This is a dry and very comfortable place to call home. At least for a few nights.

Once they are happily in this cozy den, Appleblossom clears her throat and says, "Tonight was special."

Amlet yawns, but Antonio looks interested when he asks, "Did you eat a frog?"

Before Appleblossom can answer, Amlet says, "I love frogs. Especially the legs. Were you down in the big drainpipe? I hear a lot of frogs croaking in that gully."

Appleblossom shakes her head. "No. I didn't eat a frog."

Amlet is disappointed. "Too bad."

Appleblossom struggles to find the right words. "I made a friend," she manages.

Amlet rolls over and mutters, "Who needs friends?"

But Antonio is intrigued. "Mama said not to talk to the skunks. Did you cozy up to one of those striped stinkers?"

Appleblossom shakes her head. "No."

Amlet yawns again, this time in a way that sounds too big and like he's making some kind of point that he doesn't care. "So just tell us," he says.

"The sun's coming up and we need to get to sleep. Who's your new pal?"

Appleblossom inhales deep and then exhales slowly. "I think I found a special monster."

Amlet sits up fast, banging his head on the cement block and yelping with pain. "What?!"

Antonio is even more alarmed. "Why would you find a *monster*?"

Appleblossom realizes that her big news is going over big, but not in a good way. She stammers, "I—I didn't mean to. One thing led to another."

Her two brothers are no longer consumed with fatigue. They look consumed with concern. Appleblossom can hear it in Antonio's voice when he says, "What were you even doing around monsters?"

"I went back to the same yard where I spent the day. There are good things to eat over there. I found worms and flies and snails. And even a dead mouse. I think an owl dropped him."

Amlet is easily distracted. "How was the dead mouse? Tasty, I bet."

Appleblossom manages to nod. "Yes. A bit chewy, but very nice."

Antonio isn't going to be sidetracked by a dinner discussion. "I don't care if there were dozens of dead mice. You shouldn't be spying on monsters!"

The hair on Appleblossom's back stands up. "I wasn't spying."

Amlet's voice now sounds like a growl. "This will lead to nothing but trouble."

Appleblossom tries to hold her ground. "I was thinking that both of you might want to come with me and see her. Up close. But very safe."

Antonio answers before Amlet can. "Why would we want to do *that*?"

"Research," she says in a low voice.

Amlet makes a face. "What's research?"

Appleblossom pulls her tail close to her chest and ends the conversation. "Forget about it. Good day. Sleep away."

The littlest possum shuts her eyes and hopes the discussion is over. Antonio tries to explain what research is, and Amlet moans for a while about having a headache. Antonio keeps talking about safety, but both of the possum brothers are asleep long before Appleblossom drifts off. She knows she's made a mistake telling them about the monster. She doesn't want to have secrets, but maybe that is part of growing up.

Some things, she decides, might be better not shared.

Chapter 14

It is late when Appleblossom opens her eyes the next night. She has slept in. Amlet is cleaning his whiskers and Antonio is grooming his ears. She hopes that they have forgotten about the harsh words of the night before and she tries to sound cheerful when she says, "I hear the wind. That means fallen berries on the ground!"

Antonio shoots a look to Amlet and then gets right to the point. "Amlet and I were talking while you were asleep. We don't want you spending time around people."

Appleblossom tries not to sound angry. "I'm glad that you're worried about me, but you don't need to be."

Antonio stops cleaning his ears and sighs. "We do when you exercise poor judgment."

Amlet looks confused. "What does exercising have to do with this?"

Antonio pulls on Amlet's tail. It brings him back into line, and he tells his sister, "What we're saying is important. You need to listen."

"Why does it feel like you're ganging up on me?" she answers.

Antonio's voice is firm. "We're looking out for you. That's different."

Appleblossom crosses her arms and holds them against her chest. "You're not the boss of me." Amlet snorts through his nose. It sounds mean. "Don't laugh at me, Amlet."

He turns his deep chuckle into a cough. "I wasn't. I was clearing my throat of a hairball. I've been grooming."

Appleblossom flattens her ears low to her skull. "Likely story." With that, she squeezes past the two possums and heads out into the dark as she says, "I guess I understand why we're considered solitary animals."

She hurries away from the wall, not giving them a chance to answer. She wants to get as far from Amlet and Antonio as she can. They don't understand her.

Appleblossom continues running and she doesn't look over her shoulder, but if she did, she would see that her brothers are following her. And if her feelings weren't so hurt, she would hear their rapid footsteps.

Instead, she mutters to herself, "I don't care what they think!"

It doesn't take long for Appleblossom to reach the monsters' house. She sees that the red ball is resting in the grass. and the house is dark, so she figures all of the monsters must be asleep. She heads for the ivy-covered drainpipe that runs along the side of the house and she starts to climb.

Appleblossom's brothers huddle together as they watch her reach the top of the pipe and then disappear from view. Antonio shakes a fist in frustration. "She didn't listen to a word we said!"

At his side, Amlet is equally upset. "If she's trying to act like a rebel, she's succeeding!"

"Rebels need to have causes," Antonio mutters.

Amlet adds, "And she's never even *liked* acting. She wants to just be herself."

Antonio looks up the drainpipe. "Well, maybe this is the *real* Appleblossom, and the *other* Appleblossom was just acting!" He takes a moment to consider. "That's the problem with being the actors of the animal world. How are we supposed to know what's genuine and what isn't?"

He takes hold of the vine that grips the drainpipe. "We have no choice but to follow her."

Amlet nods in agreement. "No choice."

With Amlet right behind him, Antonio works his way up the side of the house. He moves very quietly. When he reaches the roof, he peers over the lip of the gutter and sees his sister.

She is sitting on the edge of the chimney staring up at the stars. Into the pin-drop quiet Antonio calls out, "*What're you doing up here?*"

His voice startles Appleblossom. She is perched precariously on the edge of the chimney, and Antonio and Amlet can only watch helplessly as she jolts back, her feet finding nothing but air. They run to the brick smokestack, but it is too late. Appleblossom has disappeared into the darkness.

Antonio and Amlet stand for a long moment in total shock. And then they fall into each other's arms.

What has happened is not the fault of the stars. But it might be the fault of the possum brothers.

Chapter 15

Appleblossom opens her eyes.

She is alive, but in a daze. Where is she? She tries hard to make the world stop spinning as she realizes she is inside a monster house! The little possum's whole body freezes. What will become of her now? Will the large people attack? Will the dog rip her into pieces?

Anything is possible.

She waits for the assault to begin. But nothing happens. And then she realizes that the monsters are still asleep. Her tumble down the brick shaft into their lair has not disturbed the creatures. Appleblossom's body is sore from the fall, but nothing is broken.

She lifts her arms and tries to climb the sooty brick walls. But there is nothing to grip. No amount of effort will get her up the smooth sides. Appleblossom turns back to look inside the monster house. She can see all kinds of objects in the shadowy space: soft-looking nests where the people sit when they stare at their magic light box. It is now also asleep. She is afraid of that box and she wants to stay as far away as possible!

And then she hears something. It is coming from above. "Appleblossom!" "Are you okay down there?" It's Antonio and Amlet! They are up on the roof shouting down to her. Appleblossom wants to answer, but she is afraid that if she makes noise, she will wake the people, or worse, the dog. Who knows what would happen then?

She closes her eyes and forces herself not to panic. Isn't that what Mama Possum has said? *Don't panic when you have stage fright.* Well, where is Mama now? What would Mama Possum do in this situation? How should she act? They never rehearsed being trapped in a monster house.

She decides to act brave and confident. Trying out a line, Appleblossom whispers, "*If there is a way in, then there has to be a way out!*"

She's not sure she means it, but she says it a second time anyway, but with more feeling. And then she starts to move. She stays along the edge of the walls. It doesn't take long before she works her way around the largest space in the house. She finds no way out.

Up ahead is another area. She can see that this is where the people keep their food.

They store more things than squirrels! It is pos-

sible that the light boxes are telling the monsters to be hoarders. It certainly looks that way. High above on ledges she sees cartons that her nose tells her contain edible things. She spots apples in a bowl, and they are not rotten. She sees bananas and they are yellow and full, not brown with empty skins. She smells coffee and chocolate and bread and crackers and nuts.

And then her nose twitches as it detects something more overpowering than the smell of cinnamon and pepper and olive oil.

She smells a dog!

And then she sees him.

But he's in a trap!

There is a huge cage in the corner of this hoarding area. It is a square with a metal front, and inside is the beast known as Columbo. His eyes are shut. He is asleep.

It is a miracle.

And then the worst possible thing happens. The monster's snout starts moving up and down. Something bad is about to happen; Appleblossom can feel it. And the dog confirms her suspicion when he opens his eyes and stares right at her.

Appleblossom takes off running.

In the trap, the dog gets to his feet and barks as loud as anything the possum has ever heard. The noise is angry and so frightening. But then a light goes on in another part of the house and Appleblossom hears the sound of the people moving.

And somehow that is even scarier than the villainous dog.

Chapter 16

Up on the roof, Antonio and Amlet are frantic. Something is going on in the house below. Little Appleblossom must have survived the fall, because there is a lot of commotion now: They hear the dog barking, and part of the roof has lit up.

The possums run to a smooth square where there is glass instead of tile. They stare down through this window on the roof. They can see people walk by right underneath them. And they can also see Appleblossom! She is running. She turns the corner and disappears from view.

A shiver goes up Amlet's spine. "What have we done?"

Antonio shuts his eyes and does his best to concentrate. When he opens them, he is set on a plan. "We can't stay here."

"So is it every possum for himself?!" Amlet shouts.

Antonio starts for the drainpipe. "We'll come back when we have more to offer than our own limited knowledge of the situation." Amlet's head bobs up and down in agreement. "And until then, we just hope that our little sister survives."

Appleblossom's timing is perfect. She turns the corner just before a large monster emerges. A second earlier and she would have certainly been seen. The people looks in both directions, and then heads toward the barking dog. "What's going on?" the people says. "What's wrong with you, Columbo?"

One thing is very obvious: The dog named Columbo wants out of his trap. He is desperate to show what is wrong. His cage rattles and sways from the motion of his body.

Appleblossom hears the commotion, and the communication between the monsters is not good. The people's voice is harsh. "Calm down! You're waking up the whole house."

The dog stops moving. Only his tail trembles as he tries to control himself. The people looks down the hallway and then says, "Okay. All right. I'll make sure everything's okay." And with that, the monster turns in the direction of Appleblossom.

Appleblossom, for a moment, just an instant, thinks she should act dead. But then she gathers her wits and decides that if she *pretends* to die, given the circumstances, she might end up *actually* dead. Any performance right now might be her curtain call.

And so she keeps moving. She turns left. She turns right. She spins around. She stays low to the ground, head tucked down. She tries to remember acting exercises (but not the dying part). Act brave. Act the part of an animal that knows how to escape danger. And then she turns another corner and she's in a new area. She is in the place where the smallest people lives.

Up ahead she sees a nest with the littlest monster inside. Next to the nest is a pile of furry animals. Their eyes are open wide, but they don't move. She knows right away these are not real animals. They have no smell! They are fake. They are stuffed cloth.

The monster coming after her is getting closer. And so Appleblossom dives into the pile of fake furry animals—just before a beam of light sweeps into the room.

Appleblossom does not move.

She does not breathe.

She stares straight ahead and she waits. She acts like a stuffed fur animal.

The monster without much fur on his head stands in the doorway. He holds a light in his hand. This is what makes the shining beam. This hot white light spins around the room. And then it happens: The light sweeps right over Appleblossom's face. She remembers Mama saying that "an actor has to burn inside with outer ease." A famous possum named Chekhov said this. Appleblossom fixes her face in a smile. She acts fake. She acts frozen. She acts not afraid.

She thinks this might be her best acting ever.

The monster without much fur on his head stands in front of a second monster who has appeared. The second monster whispers something. Appleblossom cannot hear. And then both people turn and move back down the passageway. Appleblossom hears the monsters open the door to the house.

Then she hears the monster say, "Aha!"

Moments later, the house door can be heard closing. Appleblossom hears the biggest monster say, "Good boy, Columbo! You heard possums up on the roof. That's what it was—right, boy? I saw them just now!"

There is something about the tone of the monster's voice that makes the dog get all wiggly. Appleblossom can hear his tail thrashing against his cage. The monster continues speaking. "Well, you get a treat for that. I saw two of the nasty critters."

The word *treat* makes the beast go crazy. The word *nasty* makes Appleblossom's heart sink.

Appleblossom can hear the monster opening something in the hoarding area and then the dog known as Columbo snaps his jaws. She can make out the beast chewing. Then the people issues a command. "Go back to sleep, Columbo! We'll call an exterminator tomorrow."

The word hangs in the air: *exterminator.*

What is an exterminator?

Appleblossom thinks it through. The monster has seen Antonio and Amlet. But they must be safe, because he came right back inside. Besides, his teeth are no good for attacking. She has seen the teeth of the people: They have no points. They are flat and square and not the teeth for doing anything productive. The teeth (like their absence of tails) is another thing that must make people so unhappy.

In the distance she hears the dog named Columbo smack his lips and make a whining sound. He wants more treat. The treat seems to be all that he's thinking about now. She can tell that he has forgotten she's in the house, because she hears the beast settle back down into his cage. He is going back to sleep.

Appleblossom breathes in and breathes out and congratulates herself. She wishes she could tell her brothers and her sisters and most of all Mama Possum how she just made it past a dog and people. Her heart is pounding so hard that she can feel it in her toes, but she is suddenly more tired than she can remember ever being. There is no choice in the matter; she has to fall asleep.

But should she hide?

Appleblossom unties a hat that is on some kind of large pretend people and places it on her own head. Maybe it will make her look as if she belongs. She is surprised by how comfortable the hat is. There is a fake bear wearing a blue garment, and she pulls it off and slips it on. Her own arms fit right through the sleeves and she is able to close all of the buttons but one.

She sees that another of these fake furry creatures has black covers on its feet. She grabs one and pulls, and the funny object comes right off. It doesn't take long before she has her own toes inside both the foot covers. Her transformation is now complete. She snuggles into the pile of stuffed animals, and exhaustion overtakes her.

Moments later, she is sound asleep.

Chapter 17

Antonio and Amlet scurry away from the house. They move along the edge of the yard, wedge their bodies under a fence, and then scramble up a hill to a pile of dry, orange pine needles where it seems safe.

Amlet feels his whole body tense as Antonio wails, "What have we done?! This is nothing short of a total fiasco!"

Amlet's voice is just a whisper. "Right. Yes. But what's a fiasco?"

"A fiasco is when your sister falls down a hole into a den of monsters!" shouts Antonio.

Amlet grits his teeth. "I thought so. Yes, a fiasco, for sure. But lower your voice; we don't want the whole world knowing we're out here ready for the taking. That would *really* be a fiasco!"

Antonio grabs a handful of pine needles and breaks them in frustration over his knee. "It's our fault she fell. We frightened her."

Amlet waits for what he hopes is a respectful amount of time, and then asks, "Isn't it a *little bit* her fault? I mean, she did go up onto the roof, and we did tell her to stay away from the monsters . . ."

Antonio snorts out his long, pointy nose, and this sends several of the pine needles airborne. They lodge like pins in Amlet's chest and he cries out in pain. But Antonio doesn't even say he is sorry. Instead, he scratches the itchy spot on the top of his head and concentrates. "No. We did this. She was sitting up there and we caused her to fall.

And now it's going to be on us to try to save her."

Amlet's eyes get big. "How are we supposed to save her? I mean, really! It's not like I don't care, because I do. I care a lot. But I don't see myself as any kind of hero. It's not a part I rehearsed and it's not a part I can play."

Antonio will have none of it. "Heroes don't think of themselves as heroes, Amlet. That's what makes them heroic. We've *got* to rescue our sister. Or die trying."

Amlet can't stop himself from stammering. "D-do you mean fake dying or real dying? Are we *acting* right now or are we serious?"

Antonio's eyes narrow. "We are not acting." And then he says no more.

Chapter 18

Her name is Izzy, which is short for Isabella, but no one calls her that.

Izzy is an only child. She has long wanted a sister or a brother and when she was old enough to express this idea in the form of a strong argument, she was given a dog. She tried to name him Pal, since the plan (at least in her mind) was for the animal to be her best pal.

But her parents didn't hear her or at the very least they didn't listen, because before she knew it, the dog was named Columbo. This name sounds to

Izzy like a kind of coffee or a wild elephant. Her parents explained that this name makes the dog a detective (but a bumbling one who wears a raincoat, which makes no sense because of course the dog doesn't do that). Izzy's parents think this is amusing. She does not understand why.

Columbo is a good dog and Izzy loves him. But it is safe to say the feeling isn't mutual. Columbo's love in life (besides food, which always comes first) is his red ball. He wants to chase the thing for hours and hours and Izzy doesn't have much interest in throwing a slobbery-wet rubber toy to a dog that will then run in circles.

This leaves Izzy to sometimes feel even lonelier about not having a brother and sister than before she got the dog. And this is also because her parents spend a lot of time now on Columbo.

Columbo demands that. He wants someone

to throw him the red ball twenty-four hours a day, which of course is not possible. On top of that, he gets his hair all over the furniture, which requires a lot of cleaning. And according to her parents, he can't be trusted.

What they mean by this isn't that Columbo can't keep a secret. What they mean is that if food is anywhere within his reach, he will eat it. If you turn your back, Columbo will jump up onto the counter and bring down a plate of cookies. With one gulp he can easily swallow a whole stick of butter. He has found a way to consume an entire bag of bagels and a two-pound box of chocolate that came all the way from France. Dogs are supposed to be allergic to chocolate, but not Columbo.

The dog is, according to Izzy's grandma, "a villain." But no one in the house really thinks of him this way, although they do all admit that Columbo has successfully resisted a lot of training, which is why he sleeps in the crate in the kitchen at night. But it's a dog kennel and it's supposed to make him feel secure.

While Columbo has not turned out to be the pal Izzy hoped for, it doesn't mean that she has given up on the idea of a close friend in her home that is a pet.

She just knows the dog isn't the answer.

It is a Saturday, and that means that the regular routine of getting dressed, eating breakfast, and hurrying for the school bus can be ignored. On the weekends Izzy's parents get up when they want to and it is anyone's guess who will wander first into the kitchen and release Columbo from his sleeping crate. The dog is always immediately put outside to "do his business" (as her mother calls it). Izzy finds the whole idea of a dog doing business amusing. She can imagine Columbo putting on some kind of uniform and attaching a name tag. She sees him talking on a cellphone using a headset (the way her parents do even after they get home from work). She likes the idea of the dog sitting at a computer pretending to do business, but actually watching funny videos of other dogs.

Maybe Columbo would work in marketing. He loves anything that comes into the house in a brown paper bag. But then again, marketing (which is her father's job) doesn't have anything to do with a grocery store. When she was little, she believed that her father went shopping every day, and that someone paid him to do this. She was disappointed to learn he worked in a tall building downtown and that the *marketing* he did was for a bank.

Izzy's mother also has a job that is hard to understand. She is a chemical engineer. Engineers are people who know how to build things so that they won't fall apart. Izzy knows that math is behind the stuff they do. At least that's how it has been explained to her.

So for a long time Izzy thought that her mom told people what amount of chemical barrels were needed to construct buildings. Izzy didn't understand why anyone would want to make a tall building out of chemical barrels, but she didn't say anything. Then she discovered that wasn't what her mom was doing. She was building things made *from* chemicals—but not buildings. She works in a lab that makes different kinds of shampoo.

Izzy was shocked when she finally saw the place. It looked like a kitchen for scientists.

Now as Izzy opens her eyes and raises her arms and stretches, the house is just coming to life. She hears the door open and close to the outside. The young girl kicks off her covers and scrunches up her nose several times (which is how she always starts her day), when she decides that something in the room is different.

She senses it. Then she hears it.

Izzy stays still and holds her breath. There is a very low sound that she doesn't recognize. She keeps the air in her lungs and continues to listen. The sound is so soft, it is almost impossible to hear. It sounds like the lightest snoring in the world.

And then a second thing hits her; there is a new smell in her room.

Izzy shuts her eyes to concentrate. The odor reminds her of something. It's the smell of her thick wool sweater when it gets wet. Didn't her mom say that smell is like a sheep in the rain? It is a wild animal odor. Didn't they both laugh at that?

But there is not a sheep in her room.

And there is not a wet wool sweater.

Being as quiet as possible, Izzy rolls over onto her right hip. She stares out the window to the hedge in the yard, and then shifts her focus back inside her room. She sees her large pile of stuffed animals alongside her bed. Izzy knows this collection well. She is too old to play with these things—or at least she acts like she is if anyone else is in the room—but she still has a soft spot for all of the toys. Now, as she stares at the mound, she suddenly feels as if her heart has stopped.

Because right there in the center of the mound is something that she's never seen before. Just at her side, close enough that she could lean over and touch it, is a real animal! The furry creature has on a bonnet that belongs to an old doll, the blue raincoat from her Paddington bear, and the black boots from her circus monkey.

But even dressed this way, there is no mistaking that this animal is ALIVE. (And asleep and insanely cute.)

Izzy works hard to keep breathing. How did the little animal get in her room and why is it sleeping next to her bed? How did it come to be dressed in her toys' clothes? She isn't sure what she should do. Is this some kind of surprise? Did her parents finally understand that Columbo hasn't turned out to be a pal? Is this her real, true Pal?

And then she looks more intently at the small furry face and realizes she *knows* this creature! This is the animal she saw outside two nights ago. This is the possum that waved to her. And it all makes sense in a new way. The possum has come to be with her!

Izzy's first instinct is to go tell her parents.

Yet something holds her back. Hadn't her mother seen a small mouse in the garage a few months ago and run in a full-blown panic? Didn't a barrel-chested man named Stoffer come to the house and plug all kinds of holes with pieces of steel wool? Stoffer spoke about rodents and disease, and Izzy's mother was so worried, she took notes.

Sounds can be heard in the kitchen. Izzy's mother is awake. Her father too. But the possum does not wake. This possum is really sound asleep. Izzy takes a moment to think. The important thing for now is to keep Columbo out of her room. She feels certain that the dog will be nothing but trouble around her sweet, slumbering friend.

So Izzy slides silently out of bed. She grabs her favorite blue sweatshirt, which is slung over the back of the chair by the window, and she heads for the door. Before she leaves her room she turns to look over her shoulder.

An adorable possum with a fuzzy white face, long whiskers, and bright pink nose is sleeping with her stuffed animals. And it is the greatest thing that has ever happened to her.

Chapter 19

Izzy shuts the door to her room and moves quickly down the hall to her mom's office. She finds a piece of paper and a pen, and writes:

KEEP OUT
This means everyone!
Privacy needed today!

She then tapes the message to the door. She feels reasonably confident that this will keep her mom and dad from going into her room. Thankfully Columbo can't open doors. Izzy feels grateful (in this one instance) that she doesn't have a nosy brother or sister to worry about.

She sees her dad first. He is coming in from the backyard with Columbo. The dog looks different, even more agitated than normal.

Izzy smiles. "Hey, Dad."

Her father answers, "Good morning, Izzy," but he immediately turns back to the dog and says firmly, "Columbo! Calm down."

Columbo seems to get even more excited. His tail wags, slamming into the wall, and he bolts down the hall, nose to the floor as if he has been hired to sniff out explosives. All that Izzy can manage to say is, "What's wrong with *him*?"

Her father rolls his eyes. "We had some night-time pests. Columbo must smell them." He turns in the direction of the dog. "Settle down, boy!" But Columbo is having none of it. Izzy watches as he runs to the living room and goes straight to the fireplace. He is so excited that he uses his snout to push open the metal screen, and the next thing they know the dog is standing in the fireplace ashes.

That's when Izzy's mom appears from the kitchen. "Stop him!"

But it's too late. Columbo is now thrashing around in the chimney. He puts his paws up onto the back brick wall as his head and upper body disappear.

Izzy laughs but her mom and dad don't think it's so funny. "Get him out of there! Alex, please!" Izzy's mom is yelling now. Columbo's collar is no longer visible because half of his body is up the chimney, and then he starts barking. The sound of his deep-throated alarm echoes up the brick shaft and adds to the general sense of chaos.

And that's when Izzy notices the footprints on the floor. They are small and barely perceptible.

They head out of the chimney, not in. It figures that Columbo would be on the trail, but going the wrong way!

Izzy runs from the room, shouting, "I'll get a rag."

There is a stack of cleaning cloths on the ledge above the washing machine. Izzy grabs a handful and instead of going back to the living room (where the commotion is only getting louder), she heads straight to her room. On the hardwood floor in the hallway she can now see the trail of little sooty foot-prints. Izzy drops down to the floor and rubs them away, moving fast. All the while she hears her parents in the living room wrestling with the maniac known as Columbo.

And for the first time since the dog came into her life, Izzy is thrilled that the animal never follows an order.

Chapter 20

Appleblossom opens her eyes to a room that is bright with light.

Fear strikes like lightning and she sits bolt upright. She is locked in a monster house! In the distance she hears an enormous racket. The people are yelling. The door is shut, but for how long? Will the dog and the people come rushing in?

What is she doing out here in the open?

This is all wrong!

She needs to hide.

Appleblossom tries to scramble out of the nest of fake furry animals. But it isn't easy because she is wearing the thick blue garment. Plus she has crazy contraptions on her feet. She grabs one of the foot covers and pulls it off, throwing it hard across the room. She isn't able to get the other cover off. The hat is still on her head, and the blue garment now feels tight and constricting. There isn't time to deal with any of it!

Hurry, hurry, hurry! The words pound in her head. *Where to go? Where to hide?*

Under the little monster's nest?

Too obvious!

Under the big wooden box against the wall?

Too tight of a squeeze!

Appleblossom is running lines of dialogue, but with herself. She races awkwardly around the room, only one foot cover on, the hat flapping over her eyes, and the wooden buttons on the blue garment rubbing along the floor.

And then (in a very dizzy state) she sees a tall basket tucked into an alcove in the corner. There are all kinds of things hanging from the rim of the straw contraption. Suddenly the words of Mama Possum come back to her: "*True performers trust their gut instinct.*"

When she first heard this she had no idea what it meant. Where was your gut? And what was instinct? Mama Possum explained that your gut is the pit of your stomach. And instinct is a natural response that you know without knowing you know, and if you are a born performer in the animal kingdom (like a possum), it tells you how to play a scene. Instinct also says to never eat a wild mushroom. Or touch a black spider with a red belly. Or trust a porcupine.

Appleblossom decides that her gut instinct is telling her to get into the tall straw basket in the alcove. And so she scrambles straight to it. She grips the sides of the cylinder and it moves. She is suddenly afraid that the basket will tip over. But it only wobbles as Appleblossom climbs to the top and flings herself inside. She tumbles down through layers of cloth, soft and sweet-smelling things that she feels certain have been wrapped around the littlest monster. And then she finds herself at the bottom of the basket.

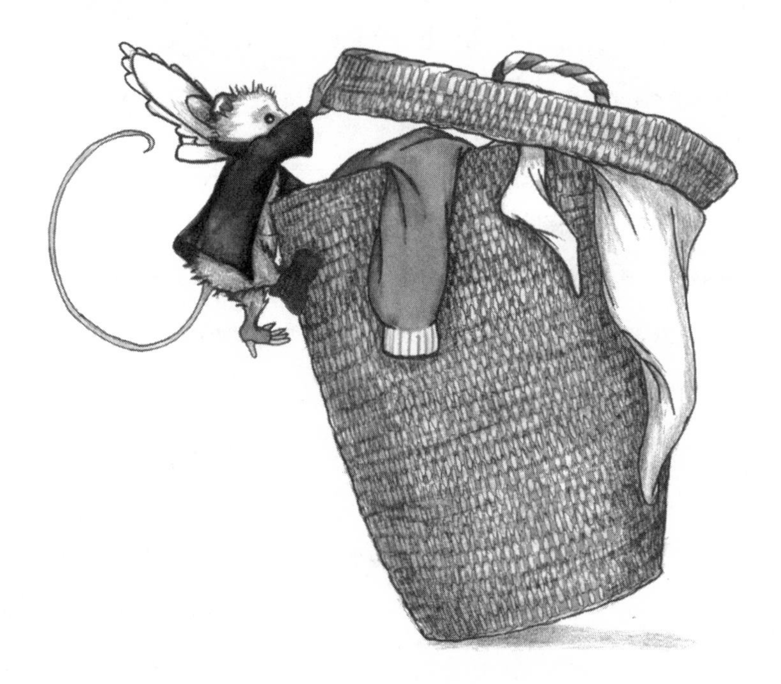

But not a moment too soon.

Because suddenly the door opens, and the littlest monster enters the room. Appleblossom stares out of a gap in the basket as the people quickly closes the door behind her. She goes right to the pile of fake furry animals.

Appleblossom watches as the little monster sucks in her breath with surprise and shouts, "Oh, NO!" She begins hunting frantically. She throws off all of the covers on her sleeping nest. She looks underneath. Appleblossom is relieved that she isn't hiding there. The people then gets to her feet and keeps searching. She tosses all the fake fur animals as she lifts everything she can get her hands on.

The mini-monster is looking for her. And then she stops. Appleblossom sees that the monster's eyes have landed on the black foot cover that she threw across the floor.

The people is staring at the foot cover, and Ap-pleblossom sees that there are tears of sadness in her eyes. They spill down her cheeks and fall to the floor.

And it's not a performance, because she doesn't know she has an audience.

Chapter 21

Izzy can't believe the little animal is gone.

She tries to stay calm. She will keep searching the room very, very carefully. She starts in the corner and goes inch by inch. She looks under cushions and all around her big chair. She moves her furniture, including the floor lamp and the bookcase. She uncovers six dead bugs, a yellow sock, a hair ribbon, and a paper clip.

The last place Izzy looks is in her closet. She moves her shoes. She pushes back every hanger (even though she can't image how the possum could get up onto the clothes). She searches the pockets of her lime-green winter jacket. Then she moves her laundry basket.

She lifts the top. She sees the pants and shirts and underwear and socks that she wore all week to school. She puts her hands in and lifts the clothing in one big clump. Nothing at the bottom of the basket.

She doesn't see the possum holding on to a pair of jeans. The mess of stuff does seem heavy, but she is tired of searching. And so she drops it all back into the basket and slumps onto the floor.

She can't contain her disappointment. One minute she had the most fantastic new pet and now the little creature is gone. And so are the bonnet for her doll, one of the boots for her circus monkey, and Paddington's raincoat.

So it turns out the possum is a burglar.

Izzy picks up the little black boot and holds it in her hands. It's like *Cinderella*. Only all mixed up.

She slips the boot into her pocket and makes her way to the kitchen, where a very wet Columbo is rolling around on the floor in a pile of old towels. The room smells like burned toast and wet dog, which isn't great.

Izzy takes a box of cereal from the counter and slides into the chair next to her father, mumbling, "So that was crazy. Columbo got pretty excited."

Izzy's mother pours herself a cup of coffee and sits down as well. "He smelled a wild animal. He knew the thing was on the roof last night. He's smarter than he looks."

Izzy doesn't say that the dog is no pet detective, even if he is named Columbo. "What kind of animal do you think was up there?"

Izzy's mom sips her coffee before answering. "Oh, we know. Your father saw them." Izzy's spoonful of cereal stops at the midpoint between her mouth and the bowl. She turns to her father. "What did you see?!"

She realizes she sounded too excited, because her father touches her arm and says, "It's okay, sweetie. We're calling the exterminator."

Izzy's mom adds: "Your father saw possums last night."

Izzy exhales. "So you woke up last night and saw a possum in the house?"

Her mother is alarmed. "Goodness no!"

Her father explains. "I went outside with a flash-light after Columbo woke us up. Spotted two by the chimney. Not big ones. Probably nothing more than babies. But *so* ugly. Like rats, only worse."

"I don't think possums are ugly," Izzy says, an-noyed.

"That's because you've never seen one. They're just the worst-looking things ever."

Izzy starts to speak again and then stops. Her little possum friend is anything but ugly. The creature has dark, shining eyes. And the most perfect nose with a pink tip. She is furry and fuzzy and smells like a wet wool sweater. But she will keep all of this to herself.

Izzy continues to chew her cereal, and then finally says, "Are you sure you need to call the exterminator? Possums are nomadic. They move from place to place. We studied them at school."

Izzy's mom is impressed by her daughter's knowledge, and her smile is one of relief. "Really? I didn't know that. So they aren't right now building some kind of nest under the house?"

Izzy grins. "No. And they don't build nests. I bet they heard Columbo and that's all it took to figure out that this was no place to call home."

Her parents look pleased.

Izzy glances over at the large, wet dog rolling on his back. He's in some kind of battle with a towel. She sees dog hair everywhere. Columbo is a shedder. That, she silently thinks, is really his greatest skill.

Izzy puts her cereal bowl in the dishwasher, then waits until her mom and dad are both out of the kitchen before she removes a small plate from the cupboard. She goes to the refrigerator and takes out cheddar cheese, four grapes, and two small carrots. She gets a sesame cracker from the box on the counter, and then adds a piece of chocolate from the secret stash in the back of the tinfoil drawer. She pours grape juice into a little cup her mother uses for hardboiled eggs. She carries all of this into her bedroom and closes the door.

Even though it appears that her little friend is gone, there is still the possibility that the possum is hiding somewhere.

And food might be just the thing to draw her out.

Izzy gets dressed and goes to the living room, where she tells her mother she wants to visit the library. Her parents are always happy when their daughter asks to spend time with books, so after the kitchen is cleaned up (and after Izzy has made sure her KEEP OUT sign is prominently posted on her door), her mom drives her down to the public library on Jensen Road. Izzy is intent on doing research. She wants to find out everything there is to know about possums.

Chapter 22

Appleblossom looks through the gap between the woven sticks of the basket. She sees the little monster come into the den and put a plate on the floor. She smells food, and feels her stomach rumble as the tip of her nose twitches.

It might be a trick!

Mama Possum said that monsters leave offerings that are really traps. The little people walks out of the room and Appleblossom waits. And waits. She hears no dog sounds. No noise from people. Through one of the cracks in the side of the basket, she can see the food on the plate. It is driving her crazy.

Appleblossom works her way up through the pile of clothing. Once on top, she balances on the edge of the basket, then swings her body around and climbs down. It doesn't take long before she is on the floor next to the plate of food.

All fear melts away at the first bite of the cheese. It's delicious. She follows with a grape. Each new thing is better than the last. Her sharp little teeth make quick work of the crunchy carrots. The best part of the sesame cracker is the dark seeds that coat the crisp offering. She drinks all of the purple liquid in the cup and it is so much tastier than muddy water! Her stomach rejoices at every new swallow of goodness, but the best comes last.

Appleblossom can't believe the taste of the dark square. Is there a way to describe this morsel of goodness? It is so sweet and smooth. It makes a green snail seem like an old pinecone seed, and every possum knows that a green snail is fantastic eating.

It isn't long before Appleblossom has finished everything in front of her. She lifts her hat-covered head into the air and considers her next move. Something sweet-smelling is close by. She knows that she should concentrate on finding a way out of the monster house, but her escape takes a backseat to her stomach, and she scurries to the area with the sweet smells.

The smells come from an area with a water chair and two empty ponds. Appleblossom climbs up a fuzzy cloth that hangs low and leads to a tube of fresh-smelling white stuff. The goop inside is delicious! It's tangy and tastes like the wild mint that grows in the fields by the stream. What a find! Appleblossom squeezes out all of the goodness. The white goo (with a swirl of red and green inside!) oozes over her hands, and she does her best to eat it up.

The next treasure is right there near the empty pond. Appleblossom pulls herself up the plastic curtain, paying no attention to the fact that her sharp nails poke small holes as she travels. She reaches a container and uses her opposable thumbs to twist the cap. It comes right off. What's inside smells like strawberries. Appleblossom scurries down to the hard white ground and lifts the large container to her mouth and takes a swig. And then . . . *ALERT. PROBLEM. BAD MOVE.*

The red goop is awful! It's not the juice of a strawberry. It is thick, foul-tasting poison. Appleblossom spits up the red slime and it comes out as a frothy mess. Her head spins. She staggers forward, moving in a weaving line around the tile floor. She doesn't notice that the red goop is all over her feet and that she's leaving pink footprints with every step.

Appleblossom does everything that she can to get the nasty sludge out of her mouth. The more she tries, the bigger mess she makes. She grabs the end of the white paper that dangles next to the wa-

ter chair. The thin tissue spins down in a seemingly endless stream, and she uses this to clean her teeth and mouth.

She burps, and pink bubbles float into the air. She's dizzy and she realizes that she's going to have trouble staying on her feet. So she wobbles back to her spot in the basket. It's a tough climb to the top, but once she reaches the rim, she happily falls into the pile of monster clothing. She then curls into a ball, pulls the hat down around her head, and holds on to her own tail. She tries to imagine that it belongs to one of her possum siblings.

And then with the taste of red slime still in her mouth, she drifts off to sleep.

Chapter 23

It is late in the afternoon when Izzy comes back into the room. She looks toward the white plate right away. All of the food is gone! This means her little visitor is still in the house. Izzy's heart starts to pound as her eyes move around the room.

She sees something pink on the tile in the bathroom, and freezes.

Is it blood?

She moves slowly to the bathroom door. The first thing she sees is toilet paper everywhere. It crisscrosses the room from the dispenser to the toilet to the sink to the tub. There is a large clump of toilet paper next to a puddle of shampoo, which is a goopy mess on the floor. The shower curtain has puncture holes in the plastic.

Izzy looks at the sink. The toothpaste tube, which had been full, is empty. The tile floor reveals something else: tracks. She bends down to more carefully examine what looks like a crime scene, and sees the prints of a shoe and what looks like a tiny, long-fingered hand. She is now an expert, and this is the track of a possum!

Izzy considers her options. She could get her mom and dad and show them the mess. They would help clean up. But would they be excited to know that her furry pal is somewhere in the house? She imagines Columbo in one of his barking fits and her parents in a full-blown panic. And so she makes a decision. She will handle this herself.

Izzy cleans up the toilet paper and the shampoo mess. She does her best to hide the punctured shower curtain by putting it on the inside of the bathtub. She throws away the toothpaste tube and wipes down the entire floor, which is covered with paw prints and boot tracks. Then she gets a book and sits on her bed.

She whispers to the room, "I know that you're in here, little Pal." She has learned (from her reading in the library) that possums are nocturnal, so she is content to wait until darkness falls to try and lure out the creature.

But weekends are the time when Izzy's parents do the laundry. Her mom and dad rotate the chores and this Saturday it's her mother's turn to do the wash. Izzy is sitting on her bed reading a book about marsupials when her mother comes in. She goes to the laundry basket in Izzy's closet and scoops up an armful of dirty clothes. She turns to her daughter. "Enjoying the new book?"

Izzy barely looks over when out of the corner of her eye she sees something. At the bottom of the heap of clothing, holding on for dear life to a pair of pants, is her possum, still wearing the pink bonnet, blue coat, and one boot. Izzy leaps up from the bed, shouting, "MOM!!!!"

Izzy's mother abruptly freezes.

The sound of her daughter's voice and the expression on her face cause Izzy's mother to gasp, "What is it?"

Izzy scrambles to her mom and tries to grab the clothing from her arms. "Give me the laundry!"

But it's not possible for her to get the whole armful of clothing, and half of it falls to the floor, including the possum. Izzy's mother sees the marsupial, which Izzy fleetingly hopes looks like a stuffed

animal, and she screams "Oh my goodness!" with the kind of alarm that would never be used about a plush toy.

She releases everything in her arms, and as she steps back, knocks into the floor lamp. The lamp crashes down and the clothing pile seems to come alive.

The clothes aren't really alive, of course, but the possum is—and it's on the run. Izzy drops to her knees and goes after the moving marsupial. But her mother shrieks, "NO! Stay back! Wild animals carry disease!"

From another part of the house, Izzy's father shouts, "What's going on in there?" And then the most dreaded sound joins the symphony of panic: Columbo. The barking dog can be heard galloping down the hallway. It is impossible to know who is more out of control. Her mother. Her father. The possum. The completely hysterical Columbo. Or Izzy herself.

Columbo charges into the room, and Izzy stops trying to catch the possum in order to lunge for the dog, grabbing his collar. Izzy's father appears in the doorway just as the possum shoots toward the bed. But Izzy's mother drops the laundry basket right over the possum, trapping the frantic animal.

Izzy's father puts his hands on the clothing basket and shouts "I got him!" which is strange because the possum is already caught.

There is nothing Izzy can do.

The cat is out of the bag. Or in this case, the possum is in the clothes hamper.

Chapter 24

So this is how it ends, thinks Appleblossom. In shadows. In darkness. Entrapped.

This is her final performance.

Her breath slows down. Her heart stops racing. And then the gland opens beneath her tail. She's in the moment and unable to control anything. She falls backward. Her eyes roll skyward. Her mouth opens. Spit comes out.

This is how a death scene is played.

Chapter 25

Izzy's father now stands right next to the overturned hamper holding a net.

He ran and got it from the garage. (It was used at some point by Uncle Randy on a fishing trip, and then abandoned on a shelf to gather dust and spiderwebs.)

Izzy's mother left the room and is now back holding a broom and a hammer, which causes Izzy to shout, "*What* are you doing with a hammer?!"

Her mother's voice is too loud. "This is just in case."

"In case WHAT?" Izzy responds. "In case you

decide that a defenseless little possum is a nail?"

Her father waves his arms in an attempt to create calm. "Okay, that's enough!"

Izzy's mother looks from her husband to her daughter. "The animal's wearing doll clothes! You've been playing with a gigantic rat!"

Izzy shakes her head. "It's not a rat. It's a possum! A marsupial. And I didn't put those clothes on her. She put them on herself!"

Izzy's parents both have uncomfortable looks on their faces, and not because of what Izzy has just said. Her father loosens his grip on the fishing net. "This net smells awful."

Izzy's mother nods. "It's like dead fish or something."

Izzy doesn't care about the bad-smelling fishing net, although she does realize that the room is quickly taking on a terrible odor. She tries to explain:

"The possum is my friend. My pal. I've seen her before through the window. I woke up this morning and she was sleeping with my stuffed animals."

Izzy's father inhales big (like he's going to hold his breath before going into a tunnel) and then exhales long. He then says, "The animal does not belong in our house. Wild animals have fleas and ticks and carry rabies. It doesn't matter that the creature somehow got into clothing. It wouldn't matter if the animal could play the piano—"

Izzy's mother interrupts: "Well, it would be amazing if it played the piano. I mean, we could make all kinds of videos and put them online and—"

Izzy's father stares at his wife. "The animal does *not* play the piano."

Izzy feels fairly certain that her possum is not musical. She doesn't want to reveal the fact that the only talent she's noticed so far is the possum's ability to make a big mess. If the bathroom is any kind of example, her new pal is an awful houseguest, so she remains silent.

Columbo has been banished to the hallway, and he is whining with a kind of urgency that is beyond any of his usual meltdowns. The dog's clear desire to sink his teeth into something other than his red ball seems to bring Izzy's parents back to the problem in the room.

Her father positions the fishing net over the laundry hamper as he instructs his wife and daughter: "You two should step back. I'm going to slowly lift the basket. The animal's going to run—"

Now it's Izzy's turn to interrupt. "We don't know she's going to run. Please be careful. She must be very afraid."

Then Izzy's father slowly tilts the laundry hamper.

They all wait.

And wait.

Nothing happens.

Finally Izzy says, “She’s not running.” Her father then lifts the hamper up high into the air, which causes the net to rise up as well. They can all now clearly see the possum.

The animal is flat on her back, arms stiff, and eyes closed.

Izzy screams, “She’s dead!”

And she bursts into tears as her heart breaks.

Her father does his best to explain as he stammers, "S-small animals can die from f-fear. They have heart attacks."

Tears run down Izzy's face. She cannot believe that the little creature is dead. But Izzy's whole bedroom has the smell of death. It's like the rotten stench of water in an old flower vase. Only worse.

Izzy's father puts his arm around her, but her mother stays at a distance. Columbo whines louder on the other side of the door. Izzy is able to say through her tears, "I want to give her a proper burial."

"Of course, sweetheart," her mother says. "We can find a nice box and we can make a place for the animal in the garden."

But Izzy continues to cry. "We can't put her out back because Columbo will dig her up. No matter how deep we make the hole." In the hallway Columbo's frantic sounds do suggest that he'd dig through the earth's core to get at this thing.

Izzy's mother nods. "You're right. We'll find a spot in the front of the house. Maybe in the rose garden. And when we see the flowers blooming in the future, we'll know that she's part of that."

It is hardly consoling news. Izzy leans close to the possum, and through her tears manages to say, "We are so sorry for what happened. We didn't mean to scare you."

Izzy's mother and father suddenly seem to feel very guilty. Her mother puts down the hammer and places the broom against the wall. "I've got a shoe box in my closet. And we have tissue in the drawer in the rec room. Nice pink paper." Izzy's father does his best to roll up Uncle Randy's old fishing net. "I'll take this out to the garage."

Izzy follows her mother to her closet, where she tries to steer Izzy toward a box that was for running shoes, but Izzy insists on a glossy black box that holds her mother's favorite high heels. Izzy returns to her room and lifts up the possum and carefully places her on top of a bed of crisp, pink tissue paper. She is surprised that the furry little animal is still warm to the touch.

Izzy's parents are standing at the door waiting. They seem very anxious to get the possum out of the house and into the hole in the ground that her father has already dug (so hurriedly that his back now hurts in places he calls the L-4/L-5 area). Her parents seem to need to have this "episode" (as she hears them whisper) over as soon as possible.

Her mother asks, "Do you want your father to take off the blue jacket—since it belongs to your bear? And the bonnet and boot?" Izzy makes a face that indicates no. Her mother manages a wobbly smile. “No. Bad idea. Also, sweetheart, it’s probably better to not keep touching the animal.”

Izzy stops crying long enough to say, “Can I have just a few minutes to myself? To say good-bye?”

Her parents exchange looks but don’t speak. After a few moments they nod and edge out of the room. Izzy stares down at the possum. She reaches her hand into the box and places it on the little animal as she says, “I’m so sorry.”

What happens next is the shock of shocks!

The possum’s little hand suddenly wraps around Izzy’s finger in what can only be described as a firm grip. Izzy starts to scream, but she stops herself.

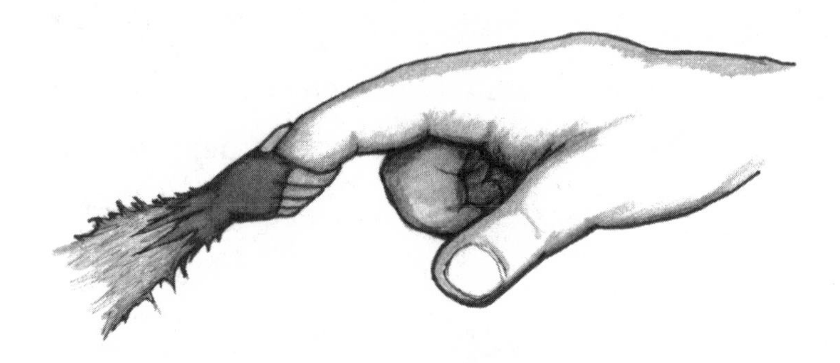

The possum isn't dead!

This possum is alive!

Izzy's eyes focus on the Paddington bear blue jacket. It moves up and down in very small increments. Why hadn't she seen this before? The animal is breathing. And then as Izzy stares into the fancy shoe box, the little possum's eyes slowly open. She looks right up at Izzy, and with an expression that can only be described as relief, her little possum mouth opens and she smiles.

It's the smile that does it.

Izzy takes action.

She scoops the possum out of the shoe box and runs to her bureau. She opens the top drawer, which is filled with soft cotton T-shirts. She then sets the possum down (she hopes in a comfortable position) and shuts the drawer. Izzy next goes to her bathroom. She grabs the shampoo bottle out of the trash can and quickly fills it halfway up with water. She tests the weight and adds another inch of water. Better.

Izzy runs back to her bed, puts the shampoo bottle in the shoe box, and pads the tissue around the container to keep it snug. She places the top on the shoe box and then grabs a ribbon from her night table. She wraps the ribbon around the box and ties it tight.

She is just finishing the bow when her bedroom door opens. Her mother looks in. "How's it going, Izzy? Are you ready?"

Izzy, no longer crying (and newly energized), tries to look sad, which is hard because she is anything *but* sad. And not an actor. She secures the ribbon and attempts to sound full of sorrow. "Yes. I said my good-bye. Let's go put her in the front yard. Right away."

Izzy lifts the shoebox and starts for the door. She hasn't gotten far before Columbo charges in. The dog jumps up to get at the shoe box. Izzy's father appears from the hallway and reaches for the dog's collar, but Columbo angles in the other direction and gallops (which is an accurate description of how the frenzied canine moves when he's focused on something) into the bathroom. Izzy's mother takes off after him. "Columbo, get out of there!"

The dog's nose goes to the ground as he frantically sniffs the floor tiles as if they are coated with beef jerky. Then, before Izzy's mother can gain control, Columbo bolts back into the bedroom. He lifts his nose into the air and Izzy can tell he has picked up the scent, because he lunges straight for the bureau. She shrieks, "Get him out of here!"

The alarm in her voice seems to penetrate the dog's brain, because he is even more anxious as he throws himself against the bureau. His claws scratch at the top drawer and his teeth clamp down on the knob! He is going to open the drawer!

But to Izzy's parents, he just appears to be an insane dog intent on destroying good wooden furniture. Izzy's father shouts, "COLUMBO! NO!"

There is something about Izzy's father's voice that commands attention, especially when he's angry. And the only thing that really gets him angry is Columbo. Izzy's father grabs the dog by the collar and pulls him away from the bureau.

Seconds later, Columbo is out of the room and sequestered in his dog crate in the kitchen.

And not long after that, Izzy and her parents lower a fancy shoe box (containing a shampoo bottle filled with water) into a hole in the front yard and say a prayer.

Chapter 26

Izzy asks to spend the rest of the day in her room. With the door closed for privacy.

Her mom and dad say yes because an animal has died and it feels as if they handled the situation poorly. At least that's what Izzy hears her parents whisper when they think she's out of earshot.

Izzy arranges apple slices, cheddar cheese cubes, poppy seed crackers, and roasted almonds on a teacup saucer, and retreats behind the closed door. She shuts the curtains that frame her large bedroom window and then makes her way to her bureau and very, very, very slowly opens the top drawer.

The possum is sitting, legs crossed, waiting for her. She stares up at Izzy and she smiles. It seems to be a shy smile, mixed with apprehension. Izzy gently reaches into the drawer, and the possum hobbles (with her one black boot) into Izzy's hands.

Izzy brings the animal to her bed and places her on the comforter. She sets the saucer of food in front of her. The possum seems eager to try a piece of apple. The look on her face shows that it's delicious. She follows the fruit with a square of cheese, a poppy seed cracker, and then all of the almonds.

And all the while Izzy watches, as happy as she's ever been.

When she can no longer contain herself, Izzy whispers, "If my parents knew you were here, I don't think they'd be pleased." The possum leans her head on Izzy's leg.

It feels to Izzy as if her heart will burst.

She has a real pal. It's as pure and simple as that.

Izzy notices that her friend has soot on the back of her legs and in her ears. Is it from the chimney? Her neck has a ring of pink fur that smells like strawberries. Dried shampoo, Izzy decides. She leans close to the marsupial and whispers, "You need a bath."

Izzy waits until the possum finishes everything on the saucer before carrying her into the bathroom. She fills the sink with warm water and gently removes the Paddington bear jacket and the bonnet and the single boot.

Izzy tries to make her voice reassuring as she carefully lowers the possum into the sink. "This is going to feel very warm and very cozy. At least I hope so. Stay calm. A bath can be relaxing and even healing. You've been through a lot, but this should make you feel better."

At first Appleblossom is afraid. But the warm water feels so good. It's as if she's floating on a moonlit cloud. She never knew that water could be this sweet. The people holds up her thumb. Appleblossom decides to show the little monster that she has a thumb too. She lifts her arm out of the water and shows her hand.

Thumb up.

She realizes that this must mean something to people, because the monster looks very happy that they both have thumbs. Appleblossom raises her other arm out of the soapy water and holds that thumb high.

She watches as the little monster squeals in a way that seems happy. She can see it is going well, so she lifts her feet out of the water.

But it's a mistake. Appleblossom starts to sink. Soapy water rushes into her ears and, when she closes her eyes, it pours into her nose. Her tail starts moving as she panics, but then two hands plunge into the water and the little people shouts, "I've got you!"

In only seconds, Appleblossom is wrapped in a small towel and held to the little monster's chest. "You're okay! I'm right here!"

What follows is a whole world of new experiences.

The little monster grabs a red machine that is attached to the wall. She aims it at Appleblossom, and it's like being in a windstorm—only a really

warm one. Appleblossom feels her fur go from wet to fluffy in a matter of seconds. And her body now smells like a field of flowers.

She has never been this clean, and her tummy is very full. Appleblossom knows she must find a way out of this place, but until the opportunity presents itself, she will act happy to be here. It is a performance that at the moment is easy to play.

Chapter 27

Antonio is restless.

He tries hard to fall asleep, but for hours he tosses and turns inside an empty flowerpot, which is where he and Amlet have finally settled as a safe place for slumber. He forces himself to keep his eyes closed, but he can't turn off his mind. No matter how hard he tries to push away the thought, there is no getting around the fact that his sister is with monsters. How can Amlet be snoring?

Antonio knows one thing: Mama Possum said

to act from your heart. When night falls, he and Amlet will do the right thing. For now he waits. And counts the hours.

Once the sun finally goes down, he presses his face close to Amlet. "Wake up," he says. It looks to Antonio as if his brother more tightly shuts his eyes. So now he's louder: "Amlet, you heard me. WAKE UP!" Amlet rolls over and his tail slaps Antonio's legs. It does *not* seem like an accident, and so Antonio *retailiates* (which is when possums use their tail for revenge): He positions his tail and whip-snaps Amlet on the backside.

The sleeping possum is now wide-awake! "Hey! What're you doing?" He spins, and now Antonio is eye to eye with his brother.

"Don't pretend to sleep!"

"I wasn't pretending!"

"Yes, you were!"

"Was not!"

"Was too!"

It doesn't take long before the two possums are exchanging more than words. Amlet grabs Antonio's ear and pulls hard. Antonio squeezes Amlet's nose. Amlet jumps into the air and comes down hard on Antonio's tail. Antonio then leaps on Amlet's back and the two possums spin around in a circle.

The fight is on!

Antonio grips his knees into Amlet's sides and grabs hold of Amlet's whiskers. He feels certain that Amlet will give up, but his brother is stubborn. He rolls out of the flowerpot with Antonio still on his back and he starts to run. He seems to hope that his brother will be thrown off by his speed.

But it doesn't work out that way. Instead Antonio releases Amlet's whiskers and wraps his arms around his brother's neck. He is now a possum cowboy. He raises an arm into the air and shouts, "Yee-haw!" (He's not sure how he knows that this is what cowboys say. In fact, he doesn't really even know what a cowboy is.)

Now Amlet seems to be in a blind rage. He kicks up his back legs in an attempt to toss his brother to the ground, but it doesn't work. He darts from side to side, but that does nothing. Then he starts running straight to the edge of the gully. Mama Possum warned them not to go down there; at different times of the year the water races through the middle of that crack in the earth.

But Antonio holds on. He doesn't believe that Amlet truly intends to go over the edge. It's just a game of chicken.

And then Amlet does the unthinkable. He runs straight over the embankment.

Antonio releases his grip on his brother's neck, but it is too late. The two possums shoot out into the open air, and for a moment, in free fall, they catch sight of each other. Their arms are spinning like windmills and their tails are swirling like the blades of an engine. Then they grab hands, scream, hit water, and submerge.

It doesn't take long before they pop up, each

safe and in one piece. They move their arms and legs like they are running, but in water, and in no time they pull themselves from the cold stream to the shoreline. They have survived. And more than that, thinks Antonio, it was strangely fun.

Once they are on the muddy bank of the creek they fall into each other's arms, hugging and laughing, out of their minds to be alive and together. "That was crazy!" shrieks Amlet. "I can't believe you didn't let go!"

Antonio sputters back, "Well, I can't believe you ran off the edge!"

Antonio and his brother hook arms and start moving toward the safety of the tall bushes, when an animal suddenly emerges right in front of them. It is twice their size, with a long nose, a mop of long, dirty hair, and large, piercing black eyes. The animal rears up on its back legs, and towers over the two possum brothers.

Antonio locks eyes with the beast, takes a sniff, and then whispers, “Papa?”

Chapter 28

This possum is bigger than Mama Possum and not nearly as well groomed. He has a big chunk missing from one of his ears and as he opens his mouth to speak, the brothers can see two things: a spotted tongue and the space where two teeth are missing.

They've never met their father, but possums have a thing called instinct. And a thing called smell. And this animal just smells like family.

"*Papa!* Who you calling *Papa*?" The imposing possum growls as he leans forward, prompting Antonio to wonder if he might attack. But it turns out the old marsupial is just moving in to get a better whiff. His nostrils flare and his eyebrows arch as he takes in a deep breath. Whatever scent they give off wipes the scowl off the big possum's face.

"Well, well, well. This is a surprise. A big, unexpected turn of e-vents," says the possum.

Antonio and Amlet both nod. They aren't certain what to think. This possum (who they now can see has long, dirty feet and a matted, oily coat) appears to be sizing them up in a new way. "You two are mine. I can smell that."

Antonio and Amlet are relieved that he doesn't look like he's going to do something extreme, like try to eat them. Instead, their father lowers himself to the ground. "I'm known around these parts as Big Poss."

Amlet finds his voice. "So is that what *we* should call you?"

Big Poss reaches out and grabs Amlet by the tail. He lifts him off the ground and swings him around in a circle. "Of course! You of all possums should call me that! You got another idea, Fur-Ball?" And with that, he lets go of Amlet, who flies through the air and lands hard.

Big Poss leans over Amlet, and his hot breath makes a small cloud in the air as he asks, "What do you answer to, small fry?"

The now-bruised possum looks up from the

ground and with a wobbly voice says, "My name is Amlet."

One of Big Poss's arms grips his belly and he laughs. "*Amlet?* Did your mother name you that?"

Amlet doesn't answer, but Antonio pipes up: "We were allowed to figure out our own names. Mama Possum is progressive."

Big Poss's eyes go wide. "So she's '*progressive,*' is she? What's that make you, little critter? The brainy baby?"

Antonio is quick to answer. "We don't believe in labels. Or bullying."

Big Poss bursts out laughing, but this time really hard. He grabs his stomach with both his hands and he jiggles from the tip of his jagged ear to the end of his thumping tail. He drops to the ground and rubs his back against the dirt. Amlet and Antonio don't know if he's scratching an itch or purposefully covering his fur in more mud, or both. "You young ones are a big surprise. So how you two ankle-biters feel about shredding for scraps together?"

Amlet perks up. "Shredding for scraps?"

But Antonio shakes his head. "We're hungry, but we've got a problem more important right now than our appetite."

Big Poss stares with a blank expression. "Is that so?"

Antonio nods. "Our sister's trapped in a monster den."

Instead of looking sympathetic, Big Poss is amused. "How'd she get trapped?"

Amlet decides to stick to the basic facts. "She was on top of a monster house and fell down a well."

Big Poss runs his fingernails through the hair on top of his head, which causes the fur to fluff up

in a wild and interesting way. "There aren't wells on top of monster houses. A well is a hole with water at the bottom."

Amlet holds his ground. "This was a big hole. I can't say if there was water below."

Big Poss continues to work on his fur-style; he runs a fingernail down the side of his scalp to form a part, and then moves a big mound of his mop forward. He's consumed with his grooming, but is able to answer: "That's called a chimney. And right now I'm thinking your mama didn't give you an education in the practical side of the theater of life. What was she doing when you were bitty babies?"

Amlet answers, "Mama saved me from an owl attack. She taught us all kinds of important stuff."

Big Poss doesn't seem impressed. "Yeah, is

that so? So what's the most important thing in the world, according to her?"

Amlet squeezes his eyes shut and forces himself to concentrate. They were taught so many things as performers. Mama said many times that they should never be afraid to make a fool of themselves by asking a question. Amlet's not sure how to say this, so he kicks Antonio in hopes that he will answer their father. Antonio's eyes meet his father's. "The most important thing in the world is family. That's why we're going to help our sister."

Big Poss spins around and gets right in Antonio's face. Even though his pointy teeth are broken and stained, they still look capable. "Is that so?"

Antonio doesn't blink. Amlet doesn't move. Then Big Poss shouts, "The wheel has come full circle: I am here! Family wins!" He tucks and rolls and then pops up on his feet. "You critters are with

Big Poss now. Follow and learn from a seasoned performer!"

Amlet sputters, "B-but what about our sister?"

Big Poss shakes his body, and bits of mud fly in all directions. Most of it hits Amlet and Antonio. "We'll see what we can do about her. What's the squeak's name?"

Antonio wipes some of the mud from his arms. "Appleblossom. She's Appleblossom the possum."

Big Poss laughs again. "We're not following a script now! This is all ad-lib." He swings around, and his hips sway from side to side. It takes a moment for the brother possums to realize that their father is singing.

Off we go, not fast not slow, looking high, looking low.

We're on a road show.

Off we move, nothing to prove, looking high, looking low.

We're on a road show.

He clicks his tongue and somehow finds a way to clap his hands, all the while making tracks as he disappears into a hedge.

Antonio and Amlet have no choice but to follow his muddy tail.

Chapter 29

Big Poss (or "Big Boss," which Antonio silently decides would be a better name) emerges onto the cement path behind a row of monster houses. He stops under a streetlight (which Antonio and Amlet both think is bold and even dangerous) and makes a proclamation: "This will be my first lesson as your Big Poss. Think of it as a master class in theater."

Amlet can't stop himself. "Mama says to avoid lights."

His father shoots him a look. "Let's not drag her into everything."

Big Poss then fluffs the fur between his ears and

strikes a pose. When he next speaks he uses a deep voice with lots of projection. "Do you know why alleys are the greatest places in the world?" Antonio and Amlet don't say anything because they aren't sure what an alley is, but Big Poss answers his own question: "Alleys have garbage cans. Now stand back. This is a life lesson. Watch the maestro perform."

Big Poss takes off in what looks like a run but has a lot of wobble and not a lot of speed. The oversized marsupial crosses the alley in this strange manner of movement, grunting as he advances. He then lowers his skull and slams headfirst into an enormous trash receptacle.

A loud thud echoes down the quiet alley. Both Antonio and Amlet gasp in shock as the garbage container rocks and then teeters and finally falls over.

But it isn't just the garbage container that goes down hard.

So does Big Poss.

The oversized possum is knocked right off his feet from the self-imposed head-on collision. Now he's on his back with his arms stretched out.

Antonio and Amlet take off across the alley. "Are you okay?" Antonio asks.

Amlet runs in a circle around the body as Big Poss's low, sad, voice moans, "I'm . . . going to . . . ask . . . you . . . to do . . . something . . . for me . . . "

Antonio and Amlet lean close. Antonio grabs his father's front paw and holds it tight. "Anything, Big Poss!" Amlet follows his example and clutches his father's back foot.

Big Poss strains to speak, causing his two sons to lean even closer. "What . . . I . . . need . . . you . . . to do . . . is . . . important . . . "

Antonio's eyes flood with tears. "Yes, Papa . . . "

Big Poss's voice growls, "It's Big Poss, not Papa . . . even to you two."

Antonio nods. "Yes, anything, Big Poss. Just tell us."

Big Poss exhales slowly and then inhales long and deep. It's a very tense moment as he makes his request: "While I'm on my back like this . . . " His voice trails out to nothing.

The two young possums wait.

And wait.

It feels as if their hearts are breaking.

Finally Big Poss finds the strength to continue. "While I'm on my back like this—RUB MY BELLY!"

Big Poss squeals as he shoots up to a sitting position. Antonio and Amlet scream. Big Poss then roars with laughter as he chokes on his words. "What a performance! Am I wrong? Who's your daddy now? Who's an actor? Who's a major star?"

Antonio and Amlet are speechless. Big Poss shoots them a harsh look. "Applause is the accepted form of acknowledgment."

Antonio and Amlet bring their hands together and clap. It's not very enthusiastic.

But Big Poss rolls over onto all fours and heads to the toppled container. "The show's over. Don't just stand there with your tails flapping in the wind!"

Antonio and Amlet watch as Big Poss grabs the plastic bag that's wedged inside the toppled receptacle. He looks over his shoulder and shouts, "Give me some help over here!" Antonio and Amlet scramble to his side and the three possums pull out the lumpy, black bag.

It smells like a real find.

Big Poss's eyes flash with excitement as he uses his teeth to rip into the thick plastic. Once he has a hole in the sack he bellows, "The world's mine oyster!" In seconds he's tossing things into piles and yelling out an inventory: "Teabag, ripped paper sack with splash of corn oil, pizza box with scraps of sausage, coffee grounds in dried filter, stale cereal, bread crusts, peanut shells, wine cork, wine cork, wine cork, moldy cheese rind, milk carton, waxed paper wrapping from butter cube, some jelly in the bottom of a jar, egg shells, toothpick, hard noodles in tangy red sauce, greasy lamb bone, carrot tops, dried peas, muffin cup with blueberry and yellow cake stuck to the sides, eggplant top, banana skin!" He then turns to his sons as he shouts, "It's a FEAST!"

Antonio and Amlet look at the contents of the plastic bag, which are now scattered everywhere. Mama taught them to be very careful in their search for food. They were told to always leave an area clean and tidy.

The two possums watch as their father's nose plunges into a glass jar. When he pulls it out, there is a large glob of marmalade on the end. It's bright orange with a curling rind of citrus that Big Poss's tongue instantly sweeps into his mouth. His lips stretch back into a toothy smile. "Don't be shy, little bugalugs!"

Antonio and Amlet make their way to the scattered heaps, and as Big Poss devours the garbage, they search for treasure to call their own.

Chapter 30

Hours later, Antonio and Amlet still haven't been able to get Big Poss's attention away from the garbage cans. Big Poss is chewing an empty yogurt container and spitting out plastic pieces when Antonio begs, "We have to stop eating and do something to help Appleblossom."

Big Poss stops spewing white chunks and looks up. Maybe he's finally full, because he says, "Your sister?"

"She's trapped in a monster house—remember?"

Big Poss's eyes narrow and he whispers, "I've

taken this time to formulate a plan." Antonio and Amlet exhale with relief, even though the plan has not been revealed.

"You have?" says Amlet. "That's great! Tell us."

Big Poss rises up on his back legs and gives his body a shake. Scraps from his meal fly in all directions. He then runs his fingers through the fur on the top of his head and works at fashioning his wild hair into his signature style.

Antonio and Amlet wait patiently.

Their father pulls on his tail to straighten it. He grabs a prickly weed from a crack in the dark asphalt and uses it to scrub his teeth. He tosses the plant, smacks his lips, and he bellows, "Are you ready to TUMBLE?"

Big Poss then springs forward and his front paws hit the ground as he kicks his back feet high into the air. His tail arches in a somewhat graceful manner as he executes a fairly decent cartwheel.

Amlet just stares, but Antonio says, "So the plan is to do cartwheels?"

Big Poss raises his arms high in the air. "Staging is very important. I thought you would have studied that in acting class."

Amlet answers with a touch of sarcasm, "Maybe we didn't have enough instruction."

Big Poss clears his throat and steps forward into the spot created by the streetlight. It's dramatic, but looks dangerous. His voice is filled with weight and importance as he delivers his message: "We must go and find your mother."

Antonio can't hide his anger. "Your big plan is to find Mama Possum?! If that was your big plan, why didn't you tell us hours ago?"

"And how do you intend to find her?" says Amlet. "We haven't seen her in days!"

Big Poss doesn't seem the least bit bothered by the fact that Antonio and Amlet are both yelling. He barely shrugs. "Oh, trust me, ankle-biters. This won't be hard. Your mother loves to hop and bop. She most especially loves to dance in the moonlight."

Antonio doesn't hide his disdain. "Mama doesn't hop or bop."

And Amlet adds: "And Mama absolutely doesn't dance in the moonlight."

Big Poss groans. "The young never really know their parents. That's the tragedy of modern life."

Amlet answers, "Of course we don't know *you.* We only met you earlier tonight."

Big Poss grabs his own tail and cracks it like a whip. "Believe me when I say that your mama loves rock and roll!"

Amlet's voice is shaky. "Hey... sure... whatever you say . . . you're the Big Poss."

Big Poss spins around and does a quick two-step. "For now, we exit, stage left."

The next thing the two young possums know, Big Poss has dropped to the ground and scurried to a telephone pole, where he starts to climb with great vigor. Antonio and Amlet have no choice but to follow.

With a lot more balance and skill than seems possible, their flabby father scrambles out onto the wires that connect the poles. Amlet and Antonio struggle to keep up. Big Poss's weight makes the telephone lines bounce, and that plus his singing make for a unique high-wire act.

The two brothers are so intent on not losing sight of the large marsupial that they forget that they have never been this far from their own neighborhood. Almost an hour passes before Big Poss finally stops, atop a pole on a platform that looks out on a wide, glowing river of light.

This is the largest cement path that Antonio and Amlet have ever seen. One side is red and one side glows bright white. Amlet whispers to Antonio, "The vicious beasts are all together."

Big Poss wraps his tail around the wire and bellows over the rumble of the metal monsters, "Take a peek at that, pilgrims!"

Antonio manages, "You took us all this way to see a monster migration?"

Amlet whispers, "What's a migration?"

Antonio doesn't answer. His eyes now fix on the wires ahead, which run toward enormous towers. These giant structures have cables strung high above the wide cement path.

Big Poss stares out into the distance. "Your mama is on the other side."

Antonio steps back in defeat. "Big Poss, I can't go out there. I have problems with heights. There. I said it. I'm a big *baby*. Maybe that should be my new name."

At his side Amlet whispers, "Same with me. Can't do it."

Big Poss looks at his two sons. "Can't do what?"

Amlet speaks for both of them. "We can't cross over the cars and trucks on the high wire."

Big Poss chortles. "We're not crossing from above. I just came to show you the view." His spotted tongue rolls back into his mouth and Big Poss turns and starts down the pole to the ground. Antonio and Amlet are both confused. If he isn't going to cross in the air, does he plan on crossing on the *ground*? Antonio calls out, "What're you doing? We can't face that many cars and trucks!"

But Big Poss doesn't answer.

Once down from the pole, Big Poss heads for a rock pile in an area thick with weeds. Scraps of paper and many, many plastic bags, mostly torn, are caught in snarls around the scrappy green shoots. Big Poss knows his way around and he moves quickly, not in a straight line but in a zigzag manner, until he comes to a large storm drain that is unseen behind the rocks.

"Follow me. Single line. And don't chase the toads. Or talk to the rats. We don't have time to listen to their nonsense!"

There is a metal grate in front of the storm drain. It isn't difficult for Antonio and Amlet to get through, but Big Poss has to draw in his breath and squeeze his body into a gap that does not look large enough to accommodate his girth. He's thrilled when he gets to the other side, shouting, "When you are an actor, your body is your instrument!"

A slow-moving stream runs down the center of the drain. Big Poss leads the way. Antonio and Amlet feel their feet slide in the ooze. It isn't long before the dark world comes alive. The first thing they recognize is the croak of toads. Amlet finds amphibians very tasty. But the three possums are full of garbage, and besides, according to Big Poss's instructions, there is no stopping now.

Antonio and Amlet hear the rats before they see them. There is a rustling noise and then the low hiss of rodent voices. "Hey there, you beasts new to the neighborhood? Can we talk? You wanna buy a snapping turtle?"

Big Poss keeps moving, but grunts in the direction of the unseen voices, "We're not buying anything you're selling!"

Several steps later, Antonio feels something hit his back. It's a pebble. He turns and sees dozens of rodent eyes. When he gasps, Big Poss rears up onto his back legs and growls, "Listen, you rats—I didn't come here looking for trouble, but I'll give it to you. I'll give it to you good!"

Big Poss then charges straight into the darkness, his mouth open to expose his forty-two sharp (but chipped and stained) teeth. But he doesn't have to use them. The dozens of rats take off in the other direction, leaving the three possums to continue on their way.

Antonio and Amlet don't say anything, but they are both impressed by the performance.

Chapter 31

The world is different on the other side of the tunnel.

There are bright lights because this is the big city.

Antonio stares at the tall structures that jut high into the sky. The trees are gone. Everything is shiny and loud (even though it's nighttime), and the air is thick with the smell of both food being cooked inside the structures and garbage overflowing from Dumpsters that line the alleys.

Amlet feels his feet tingle with excitement as

he blurts out, "This is positively a slice of possum heaven!"

Big Poss allows Antonio and Amlet to take it all in: people moving down the cement walkways, cars motoring along the wide paths. There are lights on in nearly all of the structures and the sound of machines, whirling from all directions, fills the air. The possums watch as a cart pulled by a horse appears from around a corner. The mare wears a straw hat and her oversized, floppy brown ears poke through two large holes cut on the sides. Brightly colored paper flowers decorate the horse's leather harness, and tarnished silver bells hang from a red cord that circles her neck. A white-haired people steers the slow-moving animal down the street as cars maneuver around them. It's all fascinating (and scary) to the two possum brothers.

Antonio is the first to speak. "Mama kept a lot from us."

Big Poss shrugs his shoulders. "She probably thought you weren't ready."

Amlet's voice isn't more than a whisper. "*Are* we ready?"

Big Poss finds a way to puff up his chest. "You are with Big Poss. I've got your back. But we didn't come here to sightsee. We came to find your mother. Single file. Stay in the shadows. You are supporting players. Follow the lead actor."

The young possums fall in behind as their father moves low (with his belly rubbing the smooth rock ground) out of the drainpipe. He disappears under a sleeping car. Big Poss continues (going under monster after monster) until he reaches a metal grate and slithers inside. It is dark and foul-smelling here. Amlet calls out, "Where are we?"

Big Poss keeps his voice quiet. "It's called a sewer. Hang tough."

Big Poss travels for only a short distance and then stops. Above the possums is a large circle of metal. Tiny specks of light can be seen. Big Poss stands up onto his back feet, lifts his arms overhead, and pushes. The metal lid moves and the night sky is revealed. "This way, ankle-biters!"

Big Poss pulls himself out of the sewer pipe. Down below, Antonio and Amlet rise onto their hind legs, but even standing on the tips of their toes, they can't reach.

Antonio shouts, "Big Poss! We're not tall enough!" Big Poss doesn't answer, but his tail lowers down into the darkness. The two brothers grab hold and use it like a rope.

When they get to the top, they see Big Poss gritting his teeth. "Remember that in any situation, the answer to your problem is right around you. Always. If you don't have the right props, you improvise. And just so you know—that hurt."

Big Poss then moves to a line of trash cans. "This is what we call a back alley, and back alleys are where dreams are made, ankle-biters!"

Antonio and Amlet both find the alley frightening. They see the piercing eyes of rats peeking out of crevices and they hear the sound of monsters in the buildings. They look through a half-open door and see a shelf of fire where the villains seem to be roasting animals. But the two brothers keep moving. There is no turning back now.

Big Poss is energized with every step and it is hard to keep up with his wiggly run. But it isn't long before he lets out a whooping holler and skids to a stop. Loud music comes from inside a tall brick structure. Antonio and Amlet hear people stomping their feet and slapping their hands. Big Poss points overhead to a metal staircase that is attached to the brick. "We take this to the top."

Antonio and Amlet stare. The metal staircase doesn't go to the ground. It is far, far, far out of the reach of any possum. Amlet whispers, "But how?"

Big Poss is more excited each moment. "Follow me!"

Near the staircase is a large Dumpster. Big Poss is breathless with enthusiasm as he climbs up the back, hauling his two sons with him. When they reach the top of the container (which Antonio and Amlet can see is filled with bottles and cans and half-eaten food), their father points to the metal stairs. "This is what we call the leap of faith. We're going to jump from this Dumpster to that platform. You can do it. Don't be afraid. Think of it as flying!"

Antonio sputters, "W-we're possums. We don't fly!"

Big Poss snorts through his nose. "Then think of it as falling." Without any further instruction he shouts "Geronimo!" and then flings himself out into the open air. It doesn't look like he's flying.

He lands with a loud thump on the bottom step. He then gets up and stumbles around in a circle. He's dazed. But not confused, because he hollers, "Get it done, brothers! And don't look before you leap!"

Antonio and Amlet are more than afraid. They are terrified. But what choice do they have?

Antonio turns to Amlet. "Let's do it together!" They join hands, shut their eyes, and jump.

Amlet screams.

Antonio doesn't.

But they both land right on Big Poss, which is good for them but not the greatest for the pudgy possum. He mumbles, barely able to speak, "You knocked the wind right out of me."

Antonio and Amlet feel awful. But the best thing about Big Poss (they realize) is that he gets over any emotion quickly. The next thing the two possums know, he's back on his feet giving orders and they are following him up the metal stairs to the roof. Antonio means it when he says, "Big Poss, you are the greatest actor of your generation." But Big Poss doesn't hear, or if he does, he won't acknowledge it.

The music gets louder the higher they climb.

When they near the top, Big Poss motions for them to crouch down. "You two stay here out of sight while I figure out the lay of the land. Your mother might not be that excited to see you. This place is for grown-up possums—and a few other four-footers that we tolerate."

Amlet pleads. "We're on our own in the world. How much more grown-up do we need to be?"

But Big Poss whips around and the look on his face tells Antonio and Amlet to do as they are told and keep their bellies low to the metal stairs.

Big Poss doesn't seem to be thinking about saving Appleblossom right now. His fingers are twitching and his tail is thumping, and just before he goes over the low wall onto the roof, he calls back to his two sons, "I love the nightlife! I love to boogie!"

Antonio and Amlet can't help themselves: They rise to their feet to watch. It's a sight to see. A large blinking light that looks like a green bottle is positioned on one side of the long, rectangular space. High in the sky is the full moon, casting a glow down onto the area, which is filled with dancing animals. A one-eyed cat watches from a corner and rows of bats, swinging to the beat, hang upside down on a wire that crisscrosses overhead. Moths, mixed with hundreds of fireflies, buzz directly above and they too are clearly feeling the rhythm.

Big Poss works his way toward the gyrating crowd. He gives a wave to the cat, and gets a meow back. He tips his finger to a raccoon in the corner shelling peanuts. And then just as he approaches the throng of possums, the music down below changes and Big Poss's eyes go wide. He jumps up onto a large metal box where everyone can now see him.

Antonio and Amlet are fascinated as Big Poss

holds his chin up higher than his ears and sings to the moon (and also to the raccoon in the corner eating peanuts). He moves back and forth on his hind legs, and his tail beats rhythmically in a way that seems out of his control. This much is clear: Big Poss is a major crooner.

Antonio and Amlet stare out at the crowd. As Big Poss keeps singing, the swell of animals parts to let one wiggling possum really show her stuff. The other dancing possums stamp and squeal with appreciation, and the twisting wild thing turns so that Antonio and Amlet can now see her face. Right there in the center of everything, gliding and sliding and captivating the crowd, is their MOTHER!

Chapter 32

Antonio and Amlet, eyes and mouths wide open in surprise, watch from the shadows. Their father is singing and their mother is dancing. It is both shocking and amazing.

Who are these possums?

And then the music from the monsters cavorting inside changes tempo again and gets louder. The possums suddenly all cheer! Big Poss

shouts, "They're playing our song!" He scrambles down from his spot on the box, wiggles his way out into the crowd, and grips Mama Possum's waist as he shouts, "Conga line!"

It's clear that the animals know what to do.

Mama is in front. Big Poss has her back, and a long line of possums forms from there. They take three shuffle steps forward and then stop and in unison kick up a leg on the fourth beat.

In the air, the fireflies buzz together like an electric string tossed into the sky. When it's time for a kick, they make their bodies glow bright yellow-green and fling three of their six hinged legs up toward the moon.

On the wires overhead, the bats (not wanting to be left out) draw their wings across their chests and open up on the fourth beat.

It doesn't take long before the raccoon in the corner tosses down his peanuts and heads to the end of the possum line to join in. The place is rocking! It's a sight to see.

Antonio and Amlet feel the music surge through their bodies. First Amlet starts tapping his left foot. Then Antonio finds his tail moving from side to side. The whole universe is now centered on the cavorting animals on the roof of a tall structure in the middle of the moon-filled night. Antonio and Amlet forget for a moment about their sister and they don't care anymore that they'd been told to wait for further instruction. They climb over the low wall and emerge from the darkness.

Mama Possum's head whips in their direction. She is mid-kick when she abruptly stops. The conga line behind her comes to a halt as each possum crashes into the next, causing a pileup that resembles a train wreck, but with the lone raccoon landing on top.

Mama calls out, "Antonio! Amlet! What're you doing here?" Her voice is somewhere between shocked and scolding.

Amlet is quiet, but Antonio says, "Big Poss brought us to find you."

And then the music down below ends. It has to be a coincidence, but it's suddenly pin-drop quiet.

The fireflies break out of their line.

The bats stop swinging on the wire.

The one-eyed cat darts out of sight.

Then the raccoon pulls himself up from the possum pile and, as raccoons sometimes do, speaks in a rapid and rude manner as he approaches Antonio and Amlet. "You two are wrecking a good party! Aren't you too young to be up here?"

The other possums now eye the two brothers

with deep suspicion. Then Mama Possum intervenes. "These are my sons."

Big Poss gets to his feet and steps forward. But he puffs up in a way that seems to irritate Mama Possum, because she moves right past him and heads straight to Antonio and Amlet. She sweeps them into her outstretched arms. "Come to Mama and get a hug!"

Antonio and Amlet have forgotten how wonderful it feels to be wrapped in one of Mama's hugs. There is nothing like it, really. Mama Possum always smells like an orange peel and a fir tree. Antonio knows this is because she secretly carries a sprig of fir in her front pouch. (He doesn't know why she smells like orange peels.)

She talks while she hugs them. "I want to hear what you two have been up to! How did you happen upon your father? And why are you here on the roof? You're still pretty young to be dancing in the moonlight."

Antonio and Amlet forget all about the long trek on the wires. They don't care about the rats in the tunnel or the fact that they had to jump from the Dumpster to the metal stairs. It's all worth it now because they are with Mama Possum. Antonio's head swims with thoughts. He wants to stay on this roof forever to hear music and watch the fireflies and the swinging bats and be held in the arms of his mama (which makes him sound like a baby, but he isn't). But then he remembers the reason they ended up here. "We came because of Appleblossom."

All of the possums listen. A few whisper, "Appleblossom? Who's Appleblossom?"

Amlet looks up at Mama. "She fell into a monster house. You could say it was partly our fault, but you could also say it was really just her fault because she shouldn't have been up there."

Antonio elbows Amlet. "It was an accident. But there are windows on the roof and we saw her inside. We want to try to help her. But we didn't have a plan and then we ran into Big Poss and he had a plan, which was to find you."

Amlet chimes in, "He said you'd know what to do."

Mama Possum looks over at Big Poss. He smiles, a toothy smile that Antonio thinks looks nervous.

Mama Possum stares off into the distance. It's the first time Antonio and Amlet realize that there's a good view this high off the ground. The sparkling lights of monster structures litter the horizon.

Mama Possum's hands rest on her hips and she holds her head high as she turns to the other possums. Her voice is strong and clear and forceful.

"The world believes that we are solitary, nomadic animals! But is that the case?"

Several of the possums shake their heads in what Antonio and Amlet believe means no. Mama Possum continues. "What did you experience here tonight? What's the feeling of dancing in the moonlight?"

A possum with unusually large feet calls out, "It's a ripping good time!"

Mama Possum's eyes narrow. "Yes! Yes, it is. It's one thing to dance alone, but it's something else to dance with a tribe. Especially a tribe that you understand. A tribe of possums!"

The possums are all listening now. No one moves as Mama Possum continues. "Who eats the snails? The slugs? And the rotten fruit from under the trees?"

Several of the possums shout out, "We do!"

Mama looks pleased. She is louder and more excited now, and her presentation is building. "Who takes care of the pill bugs? The anthills? The earwig nests?"

More possums join the chorus. "We do!"

Mama Possum scrambles up onto the metal box. "Who keeps the rats, the mice, and the moles in line? Who patrols the neighborhood never asking for anything?"

All the possums now shout, "We do!"

Mama Possum raises a fist into the air as she thunders, "Who is misunderstood?!"

The possums shriek, "WE ARE!"

Mama leans forward. Her voice is intimate. It is emotional. It vibrates with feeling. "Who will come with us to rescue a lost family member who has fallen into the hands of the enemy? Who will stand by our side?"

Antonio and Amlet and Big Poss are on their tiptoes. This is one memorable performance!

But the crowd is suddenly silent.

And then as fast as can be imagined, all the other possums and the one raccoon scramble off the roof and disappear down the metal stairs, leaving just Mama and Big Poss and the two young possum brothers. Seconds later, the bats and the fireflies take to the sky.

Amlet whispers, "She lost her audience."

Antonio nods. "Maybe we *are* a solitary, nomadic species."

But Mama Possum doesn't look defeated. She shrugs. "I guess it's a family production."

Chapter 33

Appleblossom sighs. Two things are certain: Being a friend to a monster is a lot of work, and nighttime is so much easier than daytime.

She has spent hours with the small people, who makes sounds that Appleblossom can't understand. At one point, the people slipped Appleblossom into a strange sack and traveled with her outside. Appleblossom believed it might be her chance for freedom. But it wasn't.

Instead, the mini-monster took one of the small screens that people hold in their hands (and sometimes hold to their heads) and she aimed it right at

Appleblossom! But before the possum could panic, whatever was happening was over and the people had returned her to the sack.

Now she is back in the house, in the monster's room. The dog is still just on the other side of the wood barrier, seemingly waiting for an opportunity to rip her head right off her body.

Finally, darkness arrives. It feels to Appleblossom as if the start of the new night holds some kind of promise.

The littlest people looks happy (but tired) as she carries Appleblossom into the area with the water chair and the empty white pond. She places soft things (that she takes from her sleeping nest) into the empty pond and then she very carefully sets down Appleblossom. "Good night, my possum pal," she says. "You sleep here in the tub. Tomorrow will be all kinds of new fun."

She then shuts the door and goes to her nest. Or at least that's where Appleblossom thinks she goes. She can't see.

Even though Appleblossom ate grapes and cheese and crispy sesame crackers, she knows now that she would take a dried-out worm, a rotten apple, and a handful of caterpillars any day of the week for her freedom. The littlest people is kind, but being a prisoner in a monster house is not the way Appleblossom wants to spend her life.

It doesn't take long before she can hear the sound (through the closed door) of the little monster breathing in that slow way that means she's asleep.

Mercy!

Appleblossom pulls herself up and looks around. There has to be a way out. Above, she can see a sliver of the moon shining down through the clear opening. How she yearns to be out in the world. She opens her mouth and all she can manage is, "Antonio . . . Amlet . . . "

But she knows it's useless. They will never hear her.

She looks upward and whispers:

"Mama, I'm stuck here.

"Mama . . .

"Ma?"

But luck isn't on her side, and the world is silent.

Chapter 34

Antonio and Amlet are relieved that Mama knows an easier way down than the metal stairs. It turns out there is a drainpipe that runs along the side of the tall structure. It isn't affixed directly to the wall and so it's easy to squeeze a possum body between the bricks and the pipe, meaning there is no way to fall.

Big Poss snorts at the idea of using this and takes the stairs anyway. "Maybe," Amlet says to Antonio, "his belly is too big to fit."

The trip back to their old neighborhood is so much shorter than the time it took to get to the city.

"It's always quicker when you know where you're going," Antonio whispers to Amlet.

Before they realize it, they are outside the house where Appleblossom fell down the chimney. The four possums gather together behind a bush and stare up at the imposing structure.

Mama Possum's nose twitches and she shuts her eyes. She seems to be thinking hard. Antonio and Amlet stay quiet, but Big Poss balls his hands into fists, strikes a pose, and shouts, "By heaven, I will tear them joint by joint, and strew this hungry yard with their limbs! The time and my intents are savage, wild, and more fierce!"

Mama Possum manages a look in his direction. "Romeo and Juliet, act five, scene three. Now sit down."

Big Poss takes a bow and returns to a crouch. Mama Possum focuses on the house. "They have a

dog. I see a red ball and I smell the monster. This is a very dangerous situation."

Big Poss stares out at the grassy yard and uncurls his tightly clenched fists. "A dog? Well, that's a different situation. We've got no chance against a dog."

Mama Possum's nostrils flare and her eyes grow hard. It's not a nice look, but it seems to change Big Poss's mind, because he says, "New idea. We enter down the chimney and hope for the best. Or we send one of our little ones here inside as a scout to report on the situation?"

Antonio and Amlet edge closer to their mother. That sounds like an awful plan. Fortunately Mama Possum agrees. "The way in is from the ground. Houses have air vents. We go in under the structure. And we go in *together*."

Big Poss turns to Antonio and Amlet. "The secret to a good relationship is to listen to your wife.

And agree with her whenever *possumly* possible." He then spins around to give Mama Possum a smile, but she's already moving.

It turns out that the house has several openings just above the ground level. They are covered by metal wire. Mama points at a vent and says, "They call this their crawlspace. But don't worry. They almost never go down under their houses to crawl. They just want to be able to. It's not clear why."

Antonio has a thought. "Monsters crawl when they are young. Maybe they maintain a romantic attachment to the idea."

Mama Possum raises an eyebrow of reflection, and then issues a command. "Big Poss, use your teeth to chew through the wire." Big Poss makes a *Why me?* face. But Mama Possum speaks again before he can object. "Your teeth are already a disaster."

Big Poss grunts, but places his snout alongside

the wire. He angles his head so that his jaw can get a good grip on the mesh. He then snaps his teeth and starts to work. The grinding makes an awful sound and Antonio and Amlet have to put their fingers in their ears. But it doesn't take long before their father has gnawed a hole in the metal weave.

From there Mama Possum and Big Poss bend back the wires. There is now an opening. Mama manages to squeeze in. Antonio and Amlet follow. And then Big Poss tries to enter. He doesn't fit.

Mama issues instructions. "Go back out and help your father." So Antonio and Amlet return outside. They push on Big Poss's backside while Mama

Possum pulls his arms. It takes a lot of effort, but Big Poss finally makes it through the opening.

They are all four now inside the monsters' house.

Under other circumstances, the crawlspace might be a place for thrills, but right now it's creepy. The first thing they all see is a rat skeleton covered in layers of dusty cobwebs. Overhead is a maze of pipes and wires.

Mama Possum leads the way. She keeps her nose low to the ground, and uses her tail to swish away the spiderwebs as she travels. The air is stale in a way that suggests mildew and mold have found the perfect home. Big Poss is the first to say it: "This place stinks. And I don't mean stinks like garbage or a pile of rotten leaves. I mean stinks like monsters!"

Amlet slows. He thinks about turning around

and leaving. He's just about ready to shout "I'll wait for you outside!" when it's too late. They have gone too far and he's more afraid to go back by himself than he is to follow his family. What a predicament!

After a series of twists and turns, Mama Possum finds what she's searching for. "Okay, this is it." Big Poss and Antonio and Amlet gather around. Mama Possum stares up at a large pipe that disappears into the low ceiling. "This goes to the monsters' heat box. And the heat box has long tunnels that lead around the house. We get to the heat box, then Big Poss will use his teeth to rip open one of the tunnels, and then we'll travel through the tunnels to find Appleblossom."

Big Poss turns to his two sons. "How does she know these things?" But he isn't asking a question. He's making a comment. And he sounds impressed.

Big Poss follows Mama Possum's instructions, and it isn't long before the wood is chipped around the pipe. Minutes later, just as Mama Possum said, they are inside a tunnel and moving through the walls of the house.

Chapter 35

Appleblossom stares up at the night sky.

The monsters are all asleep, but she is nocturnal. She shuts her eyes and her mind wanders. She hears her mother's voice, so far away, yet so present and distinctive, calling her name: "Appleblossom!"

She tries to make the voice inside her head go away, but again she hears it. "Appleblossom!" Her mother's voice is more insistent now. It keeps calling to her. "*Appleblossom!*"

This is torture.

Mama's voice continues to play tricks on her mind, and then she hears another voice. It belongs to Antonio. "Appleblossom! Where are you?"

She puts her hands to her head and sticks fingers in her ears. The voices are now harder to hear, but they haven't gone away. "STOP!" she shouts.

But the stop is some kind of go, because now she hears a new, louder voice. "That's *her*!"

She knows that voice. It's Amlet.

Appleblossom opens her eyes. Now another sound is in the mix. She hears movement coming from the wall. And then she hears a deep voice say, "Come to Papa!"

And then Mama again: "She's never even met you!"

And then: “She’ll know her papa when she sees her papa!”

Appleblossom bolts upright as she squeals, “Mama! Mama, I’m here!”

Chapter 36

Columbo looks as if he only has two thoughts in his head, but that isn't true. He has more going on than he's given credit for. Yes, his obsession with his red ball is something beyond his control. And the same can be said for his love of cheese.

But he is capable of thinking about the future. He can plot. He can plan.

And tonight, he is going to show this fact to the world.

At the end of the evening, when the boss leads Columbo to his crate, he willingly goes inside. He

doesn't whine and he does his best to look calm and in control.

But Columbo is a knot of agitation on the inside. He knows that there is still a wild animal in the house. He smells vermin and he is certain where the creature is hiding.

Izzy's room holds the enemy.

And he, Columbo, will take his opponent down.

Now, hours later, the house is finally quiet.

Do they really think that he hasn't watched them close the crate every night for over a year?

Columbo turns his skull to the side, opens his mouth wide, and hooks his jaw over the metal door. He then jerks his head up and the latch pops. Easy-peasy-squeezy-measy.

Columbo pushes with his right front paw and he is out. He stops. He shuts his eyes. He must exercise real self-control, because there is a loaf of bread on the kitchen counter and a box of stale crackers also within reach. It would be easy to get these things.

But he is on a mission and that means the food will have to wait. Something bigger clouds his obsessive-compulsive brain: the wild creature.

He knows it's a possum.

And now this possum has made a big, big, big mistake. It's in his territory. It's on his playing field.

It's about to meet the enemy.

The door to Izzy's room is closed, but that isn't a problem either. There is no lock on this door. The knob is nothing that a large mouth and a good grip can't handle. Grabbing the red ball in the yard isn't just fun and games. His lips are rubbery and his grip is firm because of practicing on that beautiful red round object.

He clamps down. He thinks of the red ball. He turns his head.

And he is in.

He sees Izzy in her bed. Asleep. The room smells of grapes and cheese and sesame crackers. It's a distraction. There may be a few crumbs from those crackers and maybe a bit of the cheese. The cheese. The cheese. Who cares about

a grape? It is nothing to him. But the *cheese*. The cheese stands alone. Every dog knows that.

Move on.

Move on.

Focus.

Block the image of the smudge of cheese and the crispy cracker crumbs. Don't think about the bread on the counter. Forget the red ball out on the grass waiting.

Concentrate on the enemy.

Inhale.

Exhale.

Do it again.

The room smells of a wild creature!

He holds his nose high. The scent is everywhere. It comes off the bed and the floor. The bureau smells, and the closet positively reeks of possum. But the strongest odor is unmistakably coming from the bathroom.

The door is closed. He goes forth. He moves slowly. But then another sense is activated. Another alarm sounds in the brain. He doesn't just *smell* the wild creature now.

He hears the animal!

Movement. Squeaks and squeals of the enemy. More than one!

Right here.

Right now.

Every muscle in his body is activated with one goal in mind.

ATTACK!

Chapter 37

They are all up against the grate. Mama Possum, Antonio and Amlet, and a big male possum she's never seen before are on one side, and Appleblossom is on the other.

Appleblossom cries with joy at the sight of her family. Mama Possum, Antonio, and Amlet are crying too. Even the strange possum is crying.

And then the stranger loosens the screws with his long, thick fingernails, and the metal barrier that separates them tips forward and they are all suddenly together inside the room.

Mama Possum says, "Appleblossom!"

Appleblossom says, "Mama, and Antonio and Amlet!"

The big possum says, "Allow me to introduce myself . . . "

But no sooner are the words out of his mouth than the bathroom door swings open and the dog known as Columbo appears.

The dog stands twenty possumids tall. His eyes flash and his nostrils flare and it is the scariest sight in the world.

They all freeze.

And then the strange possum, in a remarkably theatrical voice, roars, "By the pricking of my thumbs, something wicked this way comes!"

Amlet and Antonio hold up their hands at the dog, and Antonio bellows, "Love all, trust a few, do wrong to none!"

Amlet shouts, "All's well that ends well!"

Mama Possum rises up onto her back legs to deliver her performance. "Fie, fie! Unknit that threatening unkind brow! And dart not scornful glances from those eyes!"

Finally Appleblossom speaks the only line she remembers by the famous possum playwright known as Shakespeare: "Who ever loved that loved not at first sight?"

She knows that her delivery and performance are weak. Plus her dialogue doesn't seem to be right for the scene.

The dog seems to have had enough Shakespeare and enough stalling. It's clear that he's ready to lunge.

It's curtains for the possum family, and they know it.

This will be a tragedy, not a comedy. Not even a drama. Or a mystery.

And then Appleblossom realizes that right there in the room is a prop that might just change the way the scene plays out.

She grabs the new shampoo bottle that the people mother brought in after the other bottle went missing. It has a round red top that looks like a red ball.

Appleblossom pulls off the top and holds it out toward the dog.

His eyes lock on the object.

"Tennis ball, my liege," she says.

Chapter 38

Obsession.

The idea.

The image.

The desire.

The feeling.

One thought runs this showdown.

A RED BALL.

His red ball is outside in the grass because it's not allowed inside because a certain dog becomes obsessed and can't think of anything but this object if he sees it.

And now the red ball is here. Or a red ball that looks like his red ball.

The wild creature has it and then she throws it.

He is blinded by the light.

A red ball.

That's all there is.

Chapter 39

Izzy is up out of the bed and in the bathroom in seconds. She arrives just in time to see five possums running to the heating duct. The first one dives straight in, tucking and rolling into darkness. A second small one is at his heels. A larger possum follows with the biggest possum of the group flailing behind. Last but not least is *Izzy's* possum.

Columbo stands in the center of the room with his slobbery mouth around the red top of the shampoo bottle, which Izzy can see gave the possums time to escape. He drops the cap and lunges at Izzy's possum, but she grabs him by the collar just in time, and yanks back hard. The possum who had been Izzy's friend looks over her shoulder at Izzy and then dives into the heating duct.

Izzy shouts, "No! Come back!" Columbo wails his version of no. The only sound Izzy hears from the possum is a scurrying in the walls.

She is still in tears, clinging to Columbo, when her parents rush into the room and pronounce the dog a hero. They seem to think that Columbo has protected them from possums who were seeking revenge for the death of their friend. Izzy chooses not to tell them that the possum they buried wasn't a possum at all but a shampoo bottle.

And from now on, Columbo will not sleep in the crate in the kitchen. Instead, the dog will sleep in Izzy's room. He will take up more than half the bed. He will be allowed to have his red ball in the house. He is her protector now, or at least that's what Izzy's parents believe. And from this night onward, Izzy will have a pet. He'll be a real pal. Maybe sometimes he'll even let her put a hat on his head, or slip a scarf around his large and hairy neck.

Chapter 40

The sun is only minutes away from rising when Appleblossom and her family emerge from the vent on the side of the house.

Appleblossom hugs her brothers and her mother and she's thrilled to meet her papa. They all tail-snap and experience the general commotion that comes when a family is reunited, but then Mama Possum puts an end to it when she announces, "The sun's going to come up. We've got to go our separate ways. Remember, everyone, keep away from the monsters. Tonight was an all-star cast, but tomorrow you could stand alone. Be prepared for both!"

Big Poss agrees, adding, "If music be the food of love, play on!"

Before Appleblossom and her brothers can mount an argument that they should all stay together, at least for one night, Mama Possum and Big Poss vanish into the shadows.

The three young A-possums are now by themselves.

Amlet yawns, but it looks like he's doing it to hide the fact that he's trying not to cry. Appleblossom turns away. She wants to give him some privacy.

It isn't long before Antonio says, "Mama Possum and Big Poss don't have a lot in common, but they love the night life."

Amlet nods, adding, "And they love to boogie."

Appleblossom asks, "What's boogie?"

Antonio and Amlet both start to laugh. "You have to see it to believe it," says Antonio.

Appleblossom knows that there is a lot you have to experience to understand. But there are other things that are inside you from the start. One of them is how much her two brothers both mean to her.

The three possums climb up onto a cinder block and take a moment to just be together. They join their tails and look out at the moon. But they don't speak another word that night.

Instead, they find a hole in a brick wall along the back alley. They curl up next to one another, wedging their bodies close. Appleblossom feels a knee in her nose and a tail around her neck. She hears her brothers fall asleep as their light breathing turns to snores. She knows that while one day she might grow up to find a mate and have a family of her own, there is nothing in this world like a brother or sister.

So much of being a possum, she thinks as she drifts off to sleep, is about learning how to act. But being a brother or a sister (if you are lucky enough) is the role of a lifetime.

About the Author

Holly Goldberg Sloan is the author of three previous novels, including the *New York Times* Bestseller *Counting by 7s*, which was named an ALA Notable Book and an E. B. White Read Aloud Award Honor Book. She has worked as an advertising copywriter and a writer and director of feature films. She lives with her husband, Gary A. Rosen—the illustrator of this book—in Santa Monica, California.